IN CONSTANT FLIGHT

IN

CONSTANT

FLIGHT

stories by

ELIZABETH

TALLENT

Alfred A. Knopf New York 1983

Grateful acknowledgment is made to The Hogarth Press
Ltd. and Houghton Mifflin Company for permission to
reprint from *The Duino Elegies and the Sonnets to Orpheus*
by Rainer Maria Rilke, translated by A. Poulin, Jr. Copy-
right © 1975, 1976, 1977 by A. Poulin, Jr. Reprinted
by permission of Houghton Mifflin Company and The
Hogarth Press.

"Why I Love Country Music" originally appeared in *The
Threepenny Review.*

"Comings and Goings" originally appeared in *North
American Review.*

The following stories originally appeared in *The New
Yorker,* some in slightly different form: "Ice," "Aster-
oids," "Refugees," "In Constant Flight," "Bridges," and
"The Evolution of Birds of Paradise."

Library of Congress Cataloging in Publication Data
Tallent, Elizabeth. [date]
In constant flight.
I. Title.
PS3570.A398 I5   1983   813'.54   82-48722
ISBN 0-394-52816-6

Manufactured in the United States of America
First Edition

For Bar

Not out of curiosity, not just to exercise the heart
. . .

But because being here means so much, and because all
that's here, vanishing so quickly, seems to need us
and strangely concerns us.

RILKE, *Duino Elegies: Ninth Elegy*

CONTENTS

IN CONSTANT FLIGHT

I C E

The Abyssinian cat will not bear kittens; at some point during her pregnancies she aborts them. The veterinarian who sees her refers to these as spontaneous abortions. After the abortions the cat eats roses—yellow roses, tea roses, Seashell roses, white roses on thornless stems. My mother knows she will then find the cat, emptied of her litter, crouched on the highest shelf of the linen closet. My mother always keeps roses in her house. She is adamant about the value of certain things: old Persian rugs, McGredy's Ivory roses, Abyssinian cats. Sometimes I have seen her watch the cat doubtfully, stroking her—not with her fingertips but with her knuckles, her hand curved like a boxer's fist when his manager is lacing the gloves, at once relaxed and expectant—down the nape of the neck to a point between the shoulder blades, where her knuckles rest, having found the cat's center of gravity. The cat stares through the window. Her shoulder blades seem thinner than the bones in my mother's hands. I have seen my mother, when she thinks she is alone, examining her breasts in a mirror.

Whenever I call, she tells me first about the cat, whose nuances of behavior must be studied and reflected upon in the way that Eskimos analyze falling snow.

"Perhaps her pelvis is too narrow," my mother said the last time we talked. "Mine nearly was."

"I didn't know that," I said.

"No?"

"No."

"You don't need to worry," my mother said. "Yours isn't."

My grandmother hated cats. She is supposed to have thrown one of the earlier Abyssinians out of the window of a second-story apartment; the cat landed lightly on the roof of a cream-colored Mercedes-Benz. It was the eve of my mother's wedding when this happened. Her eyes, the next morning, were painfully red behind her veil, which my father forgot to lift before he kissed her. My grandmother was said to have given them an enormous sum of money; she wanted them to buy an island. Islands were the only way you could be sure of what was yours. In the end, she doubted everyone around her—the priest, the neurosurgeons, my mother. I remember her as an old woman who could not sleep. Once, when I went into her room to kiss her good night, she took my hand and held it to her throat, asking me whether I could feel the pulse. Her skin felt like a series of damp veils, like the wet paper you fold over the wires when you are making papier-mâché animals; it was cool against the tips of my fingers. I could smell her Chanel No. 22. "I feel it," I told her, though I wasn't sure. She was angry and thrust my hand away.

I think my mother envisioned oxygen tents and sudden intimacies, but my grandmother broke her neck falling down a flight of icy steps one evening in 1979. She had rested for a time at the bottom of the steps, one gloved hand below her cheek, the other hand (mysteriously ungloved) outstretched before her in the snow. When they lifted her, one of the ambulance men blew the snow from the deep creases in her knuckles. My mother called the undertaker to inquire about the use of perfume. "She has always, always, worn Chanel No. 22," my mother told them. Worn it, treading delicately down the centers of the icy steps, on the inside of her wrists, above the collarbones that curved like gull's wings against the cloth of her little black dress, and (for all anyone knew) in the blue-veined hollows of her skinny thighs. Before the funeral, my mother daubed Chanel behind my grandmother's ears. Her head was posed oddly on the pillow, her neck craned into a rigid, chin-upward position, the way someone will suddenly stare if you say, "Look, skywriting!" Afterward, immediately before they closed the casket, one of the neurosurgeons who had been attending my grandmother since her first stroke touched my mother lightly on the arm. "You know, she wasn't in any pain," he said. "Your mother probably never even knew what hit her."

My mother made a barely perceptible movement with her left shoulder, upon which the neurosurgeon's hand rested. No one, not even someone who was watching closely, could have called that movement a shrug.

All of this, my mother insists, was probably for the best. "In all seriousness, I don't know whether she could have endured another year," she says. The old woman sometimes forgot the names of the cats, the various species of roses; she confused the names of composers with those of television anchormen. In the last few weeks she is supposed to have taken to hiding food in her bedroom, eating it furtively at night.

And now my grandmother does not have to endure, as my mother does, the spectacle of her grandchild as a figure skater. According to my mother, skating in the Travelling Ice Adventures is only one or two extremely narrow social notches above working in an actual circus. She came to see me once, in a brand-new city amphitheater so luminous and silent that the sounds of our skates hissed back at us from the curving walls. The streets around the amphitheater had been plastered for weeks with posters advertising our coming. I could tell that my mother was shocked by my face on those billboards, two stories high.

When we spoke of the show later, over dinner, she was diplomatic. "Those lights do make your skin look odd, don't they, darling," she said. It is the lights—streaking the ice in gaudy purples, watermelon reds, deep indigo—that most people remember, not the skating. She speared a scallop with the tines of her fork, scrubbing it vigorously in the sauce. "But I did like it when you went into those pirouettes," she said. "If I squinted, I didn't really have to see the ice. I only saw you, and it looked as if you were dancing by yourself instead of with that bear."

"There's nothing wrong with the bear," I said.

"No, darling, I didn't say there was," she said. "He was very amusing."

"Whenever you unsquinted your eyes."

"I dislike glaring lights."

"It is a show. For little kids. Who *like* glaring lights."

"Of course," she said.

The bear's face is painted in an amicable grin. When we waltz, he looks out over my shoulder, grinning and nodding. The photographer used to like to photograph the bear like that, catching the line of my bare back beneath the bear's sloping jaw. For a while I was sleeping with the photographer, who travelled with us doing publicity stills for local television spots. He was a very good photographer, and he left to work for Japan Air Lines. He called me one evening from Los Angeles, where he has been taking pictures of Japanese stewardesses. They are all beautiful, he says, although he is not used to their eyes; he can't seem to bring out any reflections in them. They arrive at his studio with truckloads of kimonos; they pose with their hands in their sashes, and their skin is powdered to the color of the insides of almonds.

After dinner my mother kissed me good night; I had to catch a taxi to the airport. After the kiss she paused, her hand still cupping my cheek. I could feel her wedding ring, round and cool against the knuckle. "Roses have become my whole life," she told me. "I wish you could find something that would suit you, something you could put your whole heart into." She paused. "Don't think you know everything," she said finally. "It could happen to you. You could end up alone."

"I don't like to see you taking chances," my partner says. He is already half dressed, wearing the bear mask, which rests against his chest. His body always seems incredibly slender before he puts on the rest of his shaggy bear's outfit. Half man, half bear; I rather like him in his hybrid condition. He watches me put on my makeup, blinking at the light in my streaked blond hair. My hair wasn't always blond, but it seems that the promoters of the show cannot envision a dark-haired woman dancing with a bear—only a blond one. He lifts a human hand and strokes his dark bear's cheek softly.

"You could lose your job," he says. "They don't mind canning the women. They can't come by male skaters anymore, so they're careful, but women skaters are a dime a dozen. You've seen those girls following Harry around, trying to catch his eye."

"Harry doesn't *know* skating," I say. I choose my lipstick judiciously. If you take very good care of your lipsticks, you trim the tips with a razor blade so that they give you the cleanest line. My lipsticks are always blunt—I used some of them for years—and sometimes my mouth seems pouting and smeared. I unscrew the lipstick from its gold cylinder, I shape my mouth into a firm oval. The mirror blazes with the reflections of small blue-white bulbs; I can see the bear watching curiously over my shoulder. I am not good with the makeup tonight, and my partner notices.

"It's not whether he knows skating, it's whether you want to keep your job." He is disturbed, because, last week, I fled from him in earnest. I skated fast and hard, eluding his rough bear paws until the last possible moment, when our record was running out. When he caught me I could feel the heat of his breath on my face. The lines we had cut stretched behind us in the glossy ice. My ankles were trembling. He held me softly. No one laughed or applauded. It will not happen again.

"Of course I want to keep my job," I say. "Nobody wants to lose their job. Sometimes I antagonize Harry, sometimes he antagonizes me. That's the way it goes." I fold a Kleenex into an origami swan, which makes me think of the photographer. In L.A. there must be swans. When I was a child I made origami birds, horses, strange fish in many-colored translucent papers. My mother urged me to take up oil painting. "You're so artistic," she would say. "You should make things that will *last.*" It was true—the origami animals did not last. I lost them, or the Abyssinians tore them apart, or they blew out of windows into the street. I blot my lipstick with one of the wings of the origami swan. The bear watches me closely.

"How did you do that with just Kleenex?" he asks.

"Sometime I'll show you."

"I don't want to lose you," he says carefully. "You're a good partner; you really take it seriously. We understand each other."

"You're not going to lose me. You're stuck with me for a long while yet."

"If you could just watch it on the artistic stuff. You know how Harry feels when you get artistic. You raise his blood pressure a couple of points. He likes nice balance, accuracy, definition. You go off into a world of your own, you're lost to the rest of us, you botch the rhythms. That's what Harry sees. We try to cover for you, but he sees."

"It hasn't been that often," I say. "I've been sticking pretty close to the program, and you know you like it when I change things. You know you like it."

"All right, I *like* it," he says. "It gets so damn boring out there—all those little girls in pink birthday dresses, all the mothers in common-sense-care Dacron pantsuits. Sometimes I think they're bringing the same people in to every show—they just haven't told us. I think I recognize some of the faces. I've seen them in Toronto, in Tallahassee, in Sioux Falls. One of these days I'll just start waving at them and I won't be able to stop. The dancing bear always gets a laugh when he does anything human. That's the point. Not that he's a bear but that he's a clumsy, aborted, blotchy human being, puttering around on his ice skates with a blond woman in his arms. I can't skate without music, you know? Even in my head, when I dream about skating I hear this terrible tinny music in the background. I have to hear it before I can face the ice."

The bear's theme is played on trumpets and cymbals. He dances out into the light, he spins into a series of figure eights with his paws arching above his head, he cocks his head at the audience. He told me right away, as soon as we started working together, that he was gay, that he had once wanted to be a welder. Hundreds of little girls wave at him. He is bathed in a pink spotlight that follows him across the ice, veering and pausing skittishly.

"I know," I say. "It can get to you."

"You can't fight it," he says. He shakes his head. "Harry sees you. He's not dumb. He knows you're trying to sabotage the routines, bring the artistic stuff in. You can't go off on your own like that; the spot men don't know what you're doing. You have to stay with me, in my arms."

"I'll stay with you," I tell him. I want the bear to calm down; he seems badly shaken. His huge furry mittens lie side by side on the dressing table, like companionable Scottish terriers. I choose the small jar of plum-colored cheek highlighter. I have always had good cheekbones. The bear pulls on his arms, and then his legs. He has to fight to get his skates on; the massive bear-middle has made him unwieldy. I watch him in the mirror. The bear will court me with wit and elegance while I skate in carefully circumscribed arcs, the light shining in my blond hair. The meaning of this is not lost on the small girls who watch so intently from the bleachers.

He finishes with his skates, and although he is thinking it, he does not say "Come on." I choose an eye pencil and remove its cap.

Thoughtfully, taking great pains, I lean forward toward my reflection in the mirror and fill in the colored shadows around my eyes.

Harry watches me from the entrance ramp, keeping his hands in his pockets. Over his shoulder, the no-smoking sign glimmers purple. The narrow-hipped ballerinas sidle meekly past him, emerging one by one from the darkness into the brilliant light of the rink. I have seen Harry interview the ballerinas; he leans forward confidentially across the width of his marble-topped desk, his hands resting palm upward, beseechingly. He wriggles his fingers; it is somehow an extremely intimate gesture. His office is filled with cigarette smoke and old posters of Travelling Ice Adventures. He stares intently into the ballerina's eyes until she looks down, or away. "Are you on the pill?" he asks finally. His fingers tremble.

Now, as the ballerinas move across the ice, the beam falls through the translucent petals of their tutus. Their bare arms, held rigidly above their heads, are goosepimpled in the sudden cold. They hold their heads down shyly, watching one another from the corners of their eyes, and flutter across the ice on their skates.

"*Swan Lake* again," the bear says. "I hope to dance to *Swan Lake* at Harry's funeral."

In the darkness near us, children eat popcorn from oil-stained white paper bags, staring at the rink in a kind of ecstasy, their faces tense. Beside me the bear fidgets with one of his knees, which is loose. I have never really got used to the darkness; you skate from the shadows into the light so fast that there are always a few moments when the nerves in the retina of your eye cannot adjust, when you are skating purely by instinct.

When my mother called me this afternoon, she said that the cat had lost another litter, had vomited the petals of a Kordes' Perfecta all across the Persian rug. "I might as well give up on her," my mother said. "She will never have the temperament for it. The vet has prescribed a series of mild tranquilizers. He says it may be something in the environment that disturbs her, it may be purely psychological. But I really thought she was going to keep them this time. I just had a feeling."

"You couldn't know," I said.

"I shouldn't have forced her," my mother said sadly. "You should see how frightened she is of the toms. She just looks at them with her eyes squeezed almost shut, and then she flattens her whole body against the floor. But her face is so beautifully marked; everyone notices the shadings in the gray around her eyes. I think to myself that if she could only have kittens she would feel tranquil, that she'd adjust to them once they were born. It changes you, you know. I've never seen another like her. Now I have no choice."

"You couldn't have known," I said again. "You've been patient with her, haven't you?"

My mother paused, and I could hear the static in the background rising and falling. It sounded as if someone, not my mother, was breathing, listening impatiently to the awkward silence that had fallen between us. "Did I ever tell you that on the day your grandmother died she was running away from home?" she said softly. "The neurosurgeons had recommended confinement. It wasn't that she was dangerous, but she was badly in need of counselling, absolute quiet and rest. Somehow she overheard a conversation, and she climbed out of the window of her room."

There was a sudden fumbling at her end of the line, and a silence. "Here," she said suddenly. "I'm holding kitty up to the phone so that she can hear you. Whisper something in her ear, just between the two of you, won't you? Whisper something."

"I had a letter from Ben this morning," the bear says suddenly. "Ben is doing fine, isn't he?" Ben is my lover, the photographer.

"If you had a letter from him, then you should know how he is," I say.

"As far as I can tell, he's O.K.," the bear says. "But there is this odd tone to the letter—a disjointedness, as if he can't really make the connections, he just knows where they should be. I'm used to Ben, you know; I've worked with him for months. That's not the way he talks." He pauses, looking away from me into the brilliantly lit rink. The ballerinas skitter and regroup. They cling to one another, glittering, their bodies transparent beads fitted together on the slenderest stems.

"I don't think that anything's really gone wrong," I tell him. "It might just be L.A.—some kind of culture shock."

I can see the profile of the bear, dark and thoughtful. He strokes his cheek, clumsily now that he has his paw on. The paw has no claws—only black rubber hooks that curve down over the broad fur toes. "I don't know," he says. He is thinking hard. "He said he pulled some pictures of you from the developing fluid, and there you were. He said it occurred to him then that he was sorry he'd left."

"Why are you telling me this? Wasn't it supposed to be confidential?"

"I'm not sure about that, either," says the bear. We both hear the cymbals at the same moment, and the bear readies himself. He skates out, gliding alone onto the glaring ice, his head tilted back so that his eyes gaze upward into the crowd. There is an expectant ripple of applause. The bear bows. He moves with a dainty, shaving noise across the ice. Ballerinas file past me in the darkness, on the way back to their dressing rooms. "Damn!" one of them says. "I lost an earring. Everybody look for a small pearl earring." The ice itself is vast, the bear is a solitary misshapen figure gliding in a circle of light. He does his figure eights, and I close my eyes, following his movements on the inside of my mind. I have seen him so many times, and he always uses the same inflections, the same half-humorous, half-mocking gestures. I wait for my cue, then I appear at the entrance to the ramp. The yellow light filters through my hair, it slides in a pale aura across the ice where I am to skate, it falls from a tiny window high in the darkness above us. It brushes the ice soundlessly, colliding playfully with the bear's spot, me in my colored circle, he in his. He stares at me, pretending to be startled. The children laugh. He holds out his arms, he wags his head. My bones will show through my skin, this light is so brilliant. It is very cold. We dance, keeping the slight distance between us, me skating backward, him forward. The blades of our skates cut small curved channels in the mirroring ice, a fine powder clings to the white suede of my skates. The bear rocks forward; he catches me on one of my shy, evasive sprints, and we close and dance together, woman and bear, my blond hair against the massive darkness of his chest. His chin rests lightly on the crown of my head as he stares past me into the crowd. Suddenly, astonishing both of us, I find myself weeping in the circle of his shaggy arms.

The bear tilts his head and whispers, "You know, don't you, that you are not yourself?"

A S T E R O I D S

Ricky is in the closet, trying on my boots. There is a hole in one knee of her crimson Danskin stockings. She is long-legged for an eleven-year-old; she trips slightly, pulling on one of the boots. Soon after her mother left, Ricky began having a series of small accidents—falling down a flight of stairs, jarring the dinner table so that Joey, her father, spilled Chianti on his sweater. Once, she bruised her nose and forehead by walking into a glass door. Ricky's mother is a choreographer. After her divorce from Joey, she left for Peru, where she directs a small, impoverished corps of Peruvian dancers. When the letters from Peru arrive, Ricky shows me how they've been sliced open, the pages examined, the envelopes clumsily pasted back together. "Ricky, the llamas have tassels in their pierced ears, and the villagers get them drunk on sweet corn beer," Leigh writes. "I think I'm finally in my element." Before she got the grant to go to Peru, Leigh lived almost entirely on vitamin C, Perrier, and

Quaaludes. She is as thin and long-legged as Ricky; men sometimes stop in the street to stare after her. Ricky goes over each of the letters for hours, trying to crack her mother's secret code.

I'm taking care of Ricky because her father is my lover. Joey is an architect; he has gone to Kansas City to be with his father, who is dying. When I drove Joey to the Albuquerque airport, Ricky sat between us in the front seat. She refused to talk to him. In the airport, when she still would not speak to him, Joey began to look desperate. The guard behind the counter frowned as he shoved Joey's briefcase through the metal detector. "Come on, Mac," he said. "People are trying to catch airplanes around here." Joey picked up his briefcase. He ran his thumb across the handle. "I know it's kind of a last-minute thing," he said. "But I think the two of you should get along just fine. You'll be all right, won't you, Ricky?" A crowd of Japanese businessmen were unslinging the cameras from their necks. They were all wearing gray raincoats. Joey walked backward, still looking at Ricky. A passing stewardess smiled indulgently at him. Even if Ricky had answered him then, I doubt that Joey would have heard her. He finally turned and began to walk rapidly away, but still she did not look. She was watching the Japanese businessmen intently settling their slender cameras against their slender chests. When I touched her on the shoulder, she jumped, and one of her mother's letters fell from her jacket pocket. The smallest businessman bent lightly to retrieve it. He handed it to her and bowed. "Thank you," he said. "Thank you very much." All of the men in gray raincoats smiled in unison.

Now Ricky is trying on my Wonder Woman T-shirt; it comes down to her thighs. She pushes the sleeves up above her elbows and winds a wool scarf around her throat. Still wearing my boots, she climbs up on the bed and stares at the stuffed antelope head on the wall. The antelope's chin is inches above her forehead. His eyes are glass. Sometimes, when I turn on the light in the room, I think I see the pupils contract, although I know this does not happen. My ex-husband shot the antelope in Texas when he went to visit his sister and brother-in-law, who is an insurance salesman, like my husband. He used to come home from work, pack his pickup, and then drive all night to get to Texas, listening to the faith healers who broadcast from the Mexican radio stations. My husband always wanted children. Sometimes he mocked me, placing his hand on my head and shouting "Heal!" For a long time he drove back and forth to Texas every weekend, pretending there was nothing wrong, pretending he was only after antelope. The last weekend, he brought one home, and took me out to see the khaki-colored body in the darkness of the pickup bed; he turned on the light in the garage so that I could see it better. He had wrapped the antelope in rags. The hooves, where they stuck rigidly through the folds in the cloth, seemed sharp and delicate. The eyes were wide open; they had lashes like a woman's.

The next morning my husband drove the antelope to a taxidermist on the outskirts of town. He called from the taxidermist's living room to tell me that he wanted a divorce.

"Why are you telling me this now?" I asked.

"I just got up my nerve," he said. "There are all these heads of extinct animals staring at me from the wall, accusing me. So: we can make this an ordeal, or we can make it as easy on ourselves as possible." He told me that there was a woman in Texas, and that she had once been Miss Indian America.

"How long ago?" I asked.

"What do you mean?"

"How long ago was she Miss Indian America? Last year, or what?"

"No," he said. "It was when she was nineteen. She's thirty-two now. She has two kids, and she teaches est."

After various arguments he left me the savings account, the antelope head, the Volvo, and the duplex, which was nearly paid for. For Christmas that year he gave paperweights made of antelope hooves to each of his lover's two children.

* * *

Ricky is disappointed in the antelope. She mimics his pose, thrusting her chin forward, cupping her hands behind her ears. Joey has been gone for nine days. Today is Saturday, the morning after Halloween, and Ricky still has not taken off her mask. She stares at me through the eyeholes when I ask her what she wants for lunch. "I never eat lunch on Saturdays," she says. "Never, never. I want to go to the zoo."

"You know we can't go to the zoo," I tell her. "What if your father calls?"

"You shouldn't wait around for Joey like that," she says. "Leigh never did."

"This is different." I am not certain how much Joey has told her; I try not to alarm her. "I tell you what. You can have your choice: Stouffer's lasagna or the classic peanut butter and jelly sandwich. There isn't anything else."

"How come you never get around to doing the shopping?" Her voice is slightly muted by the mask.

"I hate to go there after work when I've been standing in front of a Xerox machine all day. My feet are killing me by five o'clock. All secretaries need to live on is yogurt, anyway."

"Yogurt is disgusting," Ricky says. "I wouldn't be caught dead eating it."

"Maybe we can get to the shopping early tomorrow." Tomorrow, I think, is Sunday. Lower telephone rates, Disney's "Wonderful World." Ricky and I have been to five movies, two art galleries, and the Mercedes-Benz dealership. The Mercedes-Benz dealership was purely wishful thinking.

"You should stop wearing those heels if your feet hurt," Ricky says. "You're probably putting stress on all of the wrong tendons." Already she has something of the dancer's pragmatism. Joey told me Leigh had taken a copy of *The Dancer's Foot Book* on the night flight to Peru. I chose the heels because I thought they made my calves look slender. (They are not.) Joey said once that he thought my motivation was deeper than that. He implied that the heels somehow matched my sense of myself. "And what is that?" I asked him. We had known each other for a couple of hours, and were drinking vodka. "Tottering slightly," he said, "and then catching yourself."

I put plates on the table and pour myself some coffee. Ricky lifts my cup, spilling a little into the saucer. Since this morning, she has been carrying a straw in her shirt pocket; she drank a bottle of Nehi orange, still wearing the mask, while she was watching "Scooby Doo."

She made the mask nearly a week ago, in an art class in school. She carried it home in a box. That day, she had stolen one of my scarves to wear to school; it was silk, and she had gotten paint on it. She seemed a little frightened, standing in the kitchen doorway. "My teacher sent you a note," she said. She took it from her jeans pocket and held it out to me. She watched while I unfolded it carefully, smoothing out the creases. It was written in pencil on a sheet torn from a small notebook. "Ricky has been more than ordinarily disruptive." That was all: one sentence, and the signature. I stared at the note; it looked as if the pencil lead had splintered at the end of the word "ordinarily." I tried to imagine the moment the lead broke, the art teacher's apprehensive start. It was possible, of course, that she didn't believe in signs. Ricky had already told me that the art teacher wore queer stockings with seams in them, that she rode a rickety bicycle to the school each morning.

"You've got to initial it and send it back with me tomorrow," Ricky said after she gave me the note. She laid the mask on the table; I saw that her fingernails were still glazed with papier-mâché glue. The mask was yellow, crimson, and indigo. It was very light, smooth inside and out. The openings for the eyes were slanting, like the narrow eyes in an Egyptian painting. I caught myself looking into them, the way you always look into a cat's mouth when it yawns.

"You did this?"

"Sure," she said. "Who else?"

"Ricky, it's very . . . It's very startling."

"You like it?"

"Yes, I do. I like it."

"I thought I'd do something different for Halloween. This will be the first year since I was five that I'm not going to be a princess. I've been all different *princesses,* you know? Blond ones, silver ones, sick ones; princesses who've been drugged by magic apples." She shrugged, looking at the mask. "No one understood what it was."

"Did you want them to?"

"No." She glanced at me coolly. "Sometimes I like it here with you. Joey would have hassled me about it for hours. 'Is it animal, or is it human? Where did you get the idea?' " She undid the buttons of her jacket and draped it over the back of her chair. She opened the refrigerator door and stood on one leg, drinking milk. She knew I disapproved when she drank milk right from the carton; it was a habit of Joey's when he was in a hurry. I started to say something, and stopped. I stroked the glazed blue cheekbone of the mask. When she smiled at me again, her curved upper lip was white with milk.

Halloween night, she came downstairs wearing the mask. It was the first time I had seen her with it on. She had wrapped three of my scarves—pink, blue, and gold—around her throat; her leotard and tights were black. There was a run in one of the legs, behind the knee. Seeing the run made me shiver. She was wearing five or six rings—the kind that come in little plastic capsules from the machines in Woolworth's. She is addicted to those machines; she will decide which capsule she wants and sometimes spend an entire afternoon trying to get it. On her left wrist she wore an old turquoise bracelet of Leigh's, on her right an ancient Timex that Joey had abandoned on my night table. Her hair was braided into perhaps a hundred tiny plaits. She looked at herself in the mirror at the bottom of the stairs, cocked her head slightly, and whistled—a brief, two-note wolf whistle. "Joey always whistles at me when I dress up," she said.

We went out. I was wearing an old black coat with the collar turned up, and still I was cold. We did not go very far. A couple of houses away, we joined a small group of children who turned and stared at Ricky. They were all nearly a head shorter than she was. A small ghost stared at her apprehensively, and backed away. The door opened and a fat woman began tossing apples into the upraised bags. A bald, middle-aged man stood at the edge of the lawn, watching the woman closely. He was chewing a long strand of red licorice, which he held in a Day-Glo mitten. When the door closed, he stepped forward and rummaged through the ghost's paper bag. The ghost turned away, embarrassed; one or two of the other kids laughed. The father lifted an apple and held it in the beam of a small flashlight, turning it slowly. "No razor blades," he said, and dropped it back into the crumpled brown bag. The other children squatted under the porch light, examining their apples.

That night, when I went into Ricky's room, she was sitting up in bed reading a Tintin comic. She was still wearing her mask. The strap of her nightgown had slid down over her thin shoulder. I pulled it up, and kissed her lightly on the hair. She made a small shrugging movement. There was a glass of chocolate milk on her nightstand, and a small plastic cube—the kind you can slide photographs into—with a Polaroid shot Ricky had taken of her mother. In the photograph, Leigh is holding a kite. She is staring at the sky with a comic, confiding tilt of her head, like a salesman's when you are having trouble making up your mind. There is a green dragon with narrow red wings on the kite. I wanted to say something to Ricky: Are you disappointed in Halloween? Is that why you're still wearing the mask? Did the kite ever fly? Instead, I sat on the edge of the bed and read a little of the Tintin over her shoulder. A small white dog moved from frame to frame, looking for something. He had black dots for eyes, but his face was somehow pointedly intelligent. Ricky read slowly. I had the feeling that she was moving her lips behind the mask.

* * *

Ricky is now wearing her Darth Vader T-shirt; her hair is un-combed, and tangles of it stick up from the rim of her mask. "La-sagna," she says. "O.K., *lasagna.*" I hear a quiet voice—it sounds as if it comes from somewhere nearby—say calmly, "You're going to have to take that thing off, you know." It takes me a moment to realize that the voice is my own. Then, since I have begun, I say, "Right now, Ricky. *Right now.*" She gives no sign of having heard. The mask tilts slightly; she must be looking out the window. When the lasagna is done she carries her plate to her room. I can hear the heels of her clogs on each stair. When she is halfway up, she pauses. "Are you sure we can't go to the zoo?" she calls. This time I do not answer. The clogs tock the rest of the way up the wooden stairs.

After what seems like a long silence, the telephone rings. It is Joey. He is in Kansas City; he says his father will not eat.

"What do you mean?" I ask. "I thought it was something wrong with his heart, not his stomach."

"Well, now he won't eat, either," Joey says. "You can see his ribs. They can't do the surgery unless he eats; he's not strong enough to survive it. And he won't eat. They're talking about starting the intravenous this evening."

"So you can't tell when you're coming home."

"Not yet. Are you angry? How is Ricky?"

"I think it would be easier for both of us if we just knew when you were coming home."

"It looks like he'll be in for a while longer. Sometimes I wish I could take him by the shoulders and shake him back to himself. The closest I get is when I'm sitting there, holding his hand. His body seems to be surrounded by a layer of extra-clear air, his own private ozone. When I was a kid, I used to think he had these huge hands. They always frightened me. Now I catch myself giving one a little secret shake, the way you'd rattle your wristwatch if you thought it had stopped." Joey's father had been a glass cutter. He had wanted two things from Joey: for him to cut glass and join a union. There was nothing on earth like the feeling a man gets from handling the big plate glass, he said. The first time he'd seen one of Joey's build-ings—it was a small jewelry store, linear and somewhat Bar-ragánesque—he had spat contemplatively on the sidewalk, and stood for a long while staring through the narrow window at the jewels.

I can hear Ricky's clogs. She is coming down the stairs.

"Ricky?" I call. "Will you come and talk to Joey?"

She is in the doorway. The mask shakes decisively—*no*.

"Christ," Joey says. "I wish Leigh wasn't in Peru. I wish my fa-ther would eat. This male nurse tried to feed him, you know, and he only got applesauce all over his chin. Damn Leigh is in another world every time you need her. She could talk to Ricky. Whenever things went wrong with Ricky, it was only Leigh who could straighten her out. It was that whole thing with Nabor that made her take off like that, I know it was."

Before Leigh had gotten her grant, she had had a lover. He was tall, with a grizzled red beard, and wore a dark stocking cap almost constantly. His name was Nabor. When he first started going out with Leigh, he was wearing a wedding ring; eventually the ring dis-appeared. They would spend long Saturday afternoons in Leigh's house watching the roller derbies on television with the sound turned off, listening to Vivaldi. Ricky hated Nabor. Often, Joey and I would take her for an evening, an afternoon, or a weekend, so that she would not have to be near him. It was not quite clear why she hated him so much; after the divorce, her mother had had several lovers, some of them even more unlikely than Nabor. Once, in Ricky's room, I saw the two of them playing with a Ouija board. Ricky sat on one side, her fingers resting lightly on the cardboard rim. The board rocked slightly when Nabor touched the pointer. His huge knees were drawn up under the child's play table. One of his shoes was untied. "Will Ricky find love?" Nabor asked. The pointer darted from his fingertips, swerved across the board, stopped at the word "No." "That's a dumb question," Ricky shouted. "I'm only eleven, for Christ's sake."

Nabor looked ashamed. He rose from the table (another man

would have teased her), and as he stood he somehow knocked a tea-cup from a doll's chest. The teacup was no bigger than a chess piece. It shattered. Ricky looked at it thoughtfully and began to cry. I don't think she cared much about the cup. Leigh was always giving her things like that, which she usually lost or traded to the other kids for something more practical: kite string, a broken ukulele, a transparency of the male body cut out of a medical book. Nabor bent and scooped the pieces of the teacup into the palm of his hand, closing his fingers around the fragments.

When the telephone rings again, in the evening, I know what is coming. I have already answered the phone when I see Ricky walking slowly down the stairs. She is wearing my long yellow nightgown, and the mask.

"What should I do?" I ask Joey. "Is there anything you want me to do here?" I find that I have wrapped the telephone cord around my wrist. "Are there people to tell?"

"I can't think of anyone."

"I just don't know what to do. There are supposed to be things I should do. I can't remember what they are."

"I'll tell you what I'm going to do," he says. "I'm coming home." When he hangs up, I hold for a few moments longer, listening to the static. In the distance I can hear the voices of two old women. They are speaking in Tewa. The sound of the language—the quickness with which they answer one another—seems designed to teach me, in useful everyday phrases, the rudiments of their language.

Ricky and I decide to go to a movie—a comedy about truck drivers. She is surprised that I tell her to put her coat on over the nightgown, instead of getting dressed again. We each wear mittens; I can barely feel her hand in mine. Ricky is wearing her mask. The woman in the booth stares at her through the glass. "You'd think she'd see all kinds of freaks this late at night," Ricky says. "You'd think she'd get used to it." I think that to see anything at all in the darkness of the theater Ricky will have to take off the mask, but I am wrong. She settles herself into her seat, adjusting the chin of the mask. I promise myself not to watch her. The man in the seat in front of us taps the toe of his cowboy boot gently against the metal seat in front of him, keeping time with a country song in the film. "This was a mistake," says the woman beside him. I eat part of a carton of caramel corn, surprised to find that I am hungry. I offer some to Ricky; she takes some, wraps it in a scrap of paper, tucks it in her pocket. She never eats in front of me now; she has become as frugal in her habits as a refugee. In front of us, the man has put his arm around the shoulders of the woman. On his forearm, just below the roll of white shirtsleeve, there is a small tattoo of a humming-bird. You can see each feather in its wings. The man's fingers curl against the woman's neck. She leans her head back against the seat, closing her eyes.

I look sideways at Ricky. The first time I ever saw her, she was wearing a black beret, and her hair was in a long braid down her back. That was before Leigh left for Peru. It was the first time Joey and I had taken Ricky anywhere with us, and I had a cold. I had been divorced for nearly three weeks then, and I had had a cold the whole time. I could tell that Joey was impatient with my sneezing. He said, "Bless you," quite carefully, each time. I looked at him above the edge of the handkerchief, while he was driving us to the zoo. Ricky was in the back, staring out the window. She held a small brown paper bag of organic sunflower seeds Leigh had given her, and sometimes she would eat some. "You don't have to say that to me every time I sneeze," I said. I didn't know him very well then. We had only gone out a couple of times; we had had supper one evening, in an Italian restaurant where the waiter did a Richard Nixon imitation while he poured the wine. Joey held the steering wheel with two hands, waiting for a traffic light to change. "I do, actually," he said. "There is an old superstition—German, I think—that if someone doesn't bless you after you sneeze, then you're going to die soon." The light changed. "I tried to get Leigh to go to the zoo with Ricky and me once," Joey said. "You know what she told me? 'The zoo is boring. All those animals.' "

At the zoo, I pretended to be entranced by the animals, most of which were sleeping. Ricky said very little. We watched a sleeping lion, his large head tilted to rest on one paw, his jaw slack, eyes slitted.

"Is he dreaming?" Ricky asked.

"Even dogs dream," Joey told her. "Cats dream. I think all animals dream."

"I know, but is he dreaming right now?"

"I don't know," Joey said. "I'm not close enough to see his eyelids. That's how you can tell. You watch his eyelids. If his eyelids are moving, he's dreaming." He was always very careful in his explanations to her. I think he wanted her to be a naturalist.

When we took Ricky back to the house, Leigh was in the kitchen. She was slowly grating cheese into a glass bowl. The steady movement of the grating made me feel even more uneasy. Leigh looked at me. She seemed only slightly curious. Joey had once described their divorce to me. "Not quite a clean break," he said. "More of a greenstick fracture." Ricky walked by me, into the kitchen. She took an orange from the counter and began to peel it. The dual gestures—grating and peeling—suddenly made the alliance between mother and daughter quite clear. That was when I sneezed into my coat sleeve. Joey turned away abruptly. He seemed to be studying his ex-wife's hands as she shook the cheese from the sides of the big glass bowl. Neither of them said anything.

After that day at the zoo, Joey called again. "I want to see you more often," he said. "It's just that there are all of these problems."

"It's O.K.," I said. "I want to see you, too."

"Often?"

"I think so."

"Can you come and play Asteroids?" Whenever he was apprehensive about things—Nabor, or his father's sudden illness—he would go to play Asteroids in a downtown bar. Asteroids is a video

game you play on a tall machine with a screen and a panel of buttons. The screen is a clear depthless black, and on it there are small
lunar-white outlines, which represent a storm of asteroids; the point
of the game is to hit the buttons fast enough so that the small ship
you are steering evades the asteroids, and to destroy as many asteroids as you can. Joey had gotten to be very good; his ship was a
small defiant point in the center of the jagged, speeding forms.
When he was teaching me, he warned me not to use the button
in the center of the panel, which would cause your ship to enter
Hyperspace, out of the line of fire; in fact, in another dimension
altogether. The problem with Hyperspace was that your ship could
explode on reentry. I was always tempted to use it, though. I think
I played more desperately than Joey; I was given to last-moment
evasions.

The following Monday, Ricky is silent during the long drive to the
airport. On the radio Carly Simon is singing "Jesse." You can see
the planes coming in over the city; Joey's flight is late, and Ricky
stands watching the runways anxiously. Without the mask, her face
seems thinner, exposed. This morning, she left the mask on her
bedside table, between the empty chocolate-milk glass and the photograph cube. She looked surprised when I said she could skip
school to meet Joey at the airport; I think she expected that I would
make her go to school anyway, as a kind of reprimand for the last
few days. Carefully, she chose a pair of painter's overalls with a
heart sewn in sequins on the bib, and a round black hat with a
pheasant's feather curling from the brim. Joey is standing near the
metal detector when we first see him. The same guard thumps the
handle of his pistol, glances at Joey, and nods. Joey looks at Ricky
and gives a long, two-note whistle. "Will you look at those two
beautiful women?" he says.

"Sure," the guard says. "Just like when you left. Been here the
whole time, waiting for you."

REFUGEES

The poet Zinbanti is tall and elegant and he was shot in the back
eleven years ago. The wound healed, of course. The doctor who,
rattling the bullet in his cupped palm, spoke to reporters after the
operation said that it had passed within a centimeter of the heart.
"Zinbanti's heart is somewhat larger than you expect to encounter,
even in a man of his height, one of the African race," the doctor
said. "It is an extraordinary heart, gentlemen, at the extreme end of
the spectrum." The journalists—there were two of them, and their
very presence in that country, in the wake of Zinbanti's escape attempt and the immediate tightening and proliferation of security,
was a kind of miracle—wrote the doctor's words down carefully,
and photographed him holding the bullet in the air. The New York
Times clipping that documents this event is now yellowing and frail;
it was tucked inside one of Zinbanti's letters to Alfred, inserted between a long description of scarabs and a short one of his second

wife. Perhaps Zinbanti has never heard of Xerox machines, Alfred thinks. Perhaps there is not a single Xerox machine in his whole country. No wonder they are always on the brink of revolution. The bullet in the photograph is in very sharp focus. The doctor, pinching it lightly between thumb and forefinger, stares at it like a child at a moth. Alfred exhales cigarette smoke, closing his eyes. It is very odd, when you think about it. Even a narrow-minded, provincial, elderly physician could be moved, when speaking of Zinbanti, to talk of hearts, of extremes, of the thread by which a life is said to hang.

For nearly a year now, Alfred has been startled by Zinbanti's letters: the angular clarity of the handwriting, the stamps engraved with sleeping lions. He began writing to Zinbanti with reluctance. Upsinger, the chairman of the English department, hoped that Zinbanti would stand as a candidate for the Telemann Endowment, which involved a series of lectures to be given at the University of Colorado at Boulder. Upsinger believed that a correspondence between poets would be the most certain way to Zinbanti's heart. Alfred wrote to Zinbanti; he was pleased with the sharpness and charm of his own letter. Zinbanti considered. He seemed to pause, falter, and retreat; Alfred, in the name of the Telemann committee, persisted. It was clear by that time that Zinbanti was the man they wanted. His newest work, *Flora and Fauna*—written during his eight years in prison following the escape attempt—had exactly the kind of slender, undaunted reputation that Upsinger was looking for. Alfred coaxed. He researched Zinbanti's life, finding old photographs of Zinbanti's village in an ancient encyclopedia: the women with their scarified brows, matchstick legs, and glossy bellies; the children combing fallen grains of wheat from the dust with knobby fingers. Alfred called Zinbanti. The connections were invariably riddled with static, and Zinbanti proved extremely telephone-shy. When he finally agreed—one night after Alfred had been talking into the rise and fall of static for nearly forty minutes—to accept the Telemann Endowment, Alfred got drunk on

Gordon's gin, which he somehow associated with Africa. He woke in the dead of night with a feeling of confused urgency; he had been dreaming of escaping in a helicopter from a barren, level country that, even in the dream, he knew he did not recognize.

Now, lying on his bed, he thinks of that country. There was a single highway, ashen and gray, immaculate as only highways that cross immense deserts can be. There were no lines on the highway. Alfred stares at the ceiling. He is smoking one of Lisa's cigarettes; when they were living together, he used to steal them from the pocket of her russet suede jacket whenever they were in movie theaters. She is the only woman he has ever known who keeps cigarettes in her pockets. This cigarette he stole during *The Last Métro*. In the darkness, she misinterpreted the lightness of his touch. "Christ, Alfred," she said. "Can't you even wait until the cartoon is over?" She is married; they went to movies often. "I'm not psychologically equipped to have a lover," she said the last time. "Really. You don't believe me?" "No," he said. Once, when she buried her hand in the popcorn carton—grainy cardboard printed with shooting stars—he kissed the butter from her knuckles. Her hand had gotten so slick with butter that her wedding ring had slid from her finger to the bottom of the carton. "Like a Cracker Jack prize," Alfred said.

"It's not funny, Alfred," she said. Without looking at him, she slipped the buttery ring deep into the bottom of her russet suede pocket.

He has also taken one of Lisa's gray suede Italian gloves; this he intends to return. The glove rests on his bedside table, palm upward, fingers innocently curved. When she calls him in the middle of the night—which she often does—her voice is guarded, as if in preparation for his pleading, his reproaches. There is a small gray feather, which he found on a windowsill, cupped in the palm of the glove.

*   *   *

"Think of it as if you are taking in a refugee," Lisa had told him when she moved in six weeks ago. "Think of me as a sort of boat person." She opened the door of his refrigerator and stood on one leg, staring into the interior. Her leg was long and thin. One bare foot rested lightly behind the knee of the other leg. "Haven't you got anything to eat? What do you do, collect old jars of mayonnaise?"

"You're in exile," he said.

"I know," she said. "Jacob has probably taken a contract out on me by now. I'm the object of a lot of redirected aggression, you know? Jacob's very ambitious about his career. He's virtually a second Konrad Lorenz. It's not easy to love a second Konrad Lorenz—not unless you're a graylag goose. Alfred, I count five jars of mayonnaise in here."

"Would you like an egg-salad sandwich?"

"God, no," she said.

Then, two weeks ago, Lisa left him, packing her things in a bag made of parachute silk. She was not exactly going back to her husband, she said. It was just that her husband, although ambitious, is also tranquil and that right now, at this point in her life, she is extremely interested in tranquility in men.

"It used to be the other way around," Alfred said. "Men were interested in tranquility in women."

"Times change," she said. "I can't help it, Alfred. It attracts me."

"Of course he's tranquil," Alfred said. "He's had all of this time without you—time to do nothing but chart flights of migratory songbirds. I could be tranquil, too, if my primary interest in life was the flight of the scarlet tanager."

"I doubt it," she said. "I doubt you'd be tranquil, even then. Look what a mess your psyche is in over this Zinbanti negotiation."

She was sitting up in bed, with the quilt drawn up around her knees. She was always cold in the apartment; they often fought over the thermostat. He could see the slenderness of her knees below the quilt.

"Now it's all changed around," she said.

"Now what is all changed around?"

"The air of tranquility you used to have. It's gone. You've lost it."

"I could get it back."

"You can't. It's Zinbanti. Your eyes, the way you *narrow* them whenever I say his name. You hate Zinbanti."

"I don't hate Zinbanti."

"You're a very distracted man, Alfred."

Because Lisa and Alfred were both on the Telemann committee, they had watched a number of films of Zinbanti reading from his works. He is oddly photogenic. He has a long throat, slender sloping shoulders, and a slight concavity—like that of a basketball player—at the base of the spine, detectable even beneath his suit coat. But the wound seemed to have left in Zinbanti something of the shade of premonition you can see in the eyes of antelope, in which the iris seems too large for the eye, overshadowing the white. He will not lecture in a place where he cannot have his back to the wall. In fact, Zinbanti walks with the slightest of shrugs, his shoulder blades contracting and flaring with each step. Alfred had observed the shrug in film clips and pointed it out to Lisa. "That shrug is to Zinbanti what tousled white hair was to Frost," he told her. Lisa did not seem to be listening. She was staring at the screen; her eyes were wide. In the splintering sunlight of an African noon, Zinbanti was reading a poem called "Onyx." "It's very interesting to interpret that shrug psychologically," Alfred said. "Zinbanti knows that each time he appears in public he is vulnerable, and with each step he takes, he shrugs at the danger."

Lisa did not turn her head. She continued to stare at the screen.

"Then again," Alfred said, "it may be only some sort of complicated tendon damage."

"Alfred," Lisa said. "You're gray with jealousy."

He was startled. "Of what?" he said. "Of Zinbanti?"

"Listen to the way you talk about him, sometime."

"What's wrong with the way I talk about him?"

"You have this *aggrieved* tone. You're worse than Upsinger. Upsinger adopts this self-reproachful humility. You're so isolated, all of you. You can't comprehend Zinbanti because you have no interaction with the land, the light, other species—"

"To tell you the truth," he said, "the only other species that interests me right now is you."

"I'm not another species."

"In some ways you are," he said. "I think it's green, by the way."

"What is green?"

"Green with jealousy. Not gray."

She stared straight ahead. On the narrow screen, Zinbanti nodded politely to an invisible audience. His cheekbones gleamed like amber.

Now Alfred turns on his side; the quilt is rumpled and he smooths it carefully. He dials the telephone number of Lisa's husband's duplex. The telephone rings fifteen times. He imagines that each of the rings has a peculiar airiness, as if the ceilings of the duplex were very high.

"How long were you going to let it ring?" he says.

"I don't know," she says. "How long were you?"

"What are you eating, a salami sandwich?" She had once had a fierce love for salami sandwiches. She ate them even in bed. In the mornings her breath tasted poignantly of salami.

"No," she says. "Grilled cheese."

"Can you come to the airport in the morning?"

"Is this to get Zinbanti?"

"Yes," Alfred says. "He gets in at five-twenty."

"That's awfully early," she says. "All right."

"I'll see you."

"Alfred," she says. "Don't go around hanging your hat on a ghost."

"What?"

"It's a proverb."

"What kind of proverb?"

She hangs up. He holds the telephone next to his ear, hoping she will pick it up again. A tiny, reproving voice comes onto the line, urging him to replace the receiver in its cradle.

It is still dark when she meets him in the doorway of the duplex. She is wearing an ancient kimono, sashed with one of her husband's neckties, and a pair of white suede cowboy boots. There are no lights on in the house behind her.

"Where's Jacob?" he says.

She looks at him, tilting her chin. "He's in the field," she says.

"What field?"

"Field," she says. "As in *field* work."

"I know," he says. "Where is the field?"

"Oh," she says. "Michigan." He follows her into the dark kitchen, which he has never seen before. She turns on the light. The kitchen is utterly bare, except for a single stack of Oreos on the pink linoleum counter. Lisa is running water into a battered coffeepot.

"He won't let me use this one while he's here," she says. "I threw it against the wall the first week we were married. He hates it. He says he keeps hearing the bang it made against the white plaster wall." She holds the coffeepot up. Alfred looks at it closely.

"What is he doing in Michigan?" Alfred asks.

"I don't know," she says. "He's got some orchard staked out. Little tape recorders camouflaged by leaves. He's recording orioles."

"You didn't tell me he was gone."

"I didn't know exactly what I was getting into," she says. "It just seems to me now that there ought to be a sort of interval between a husband and a lover—"

"Interval?"

"A sort of white space," she says.

"Can we go to bed?"

"No," she says. "We can have coffee. Then we can drive to the airport to get Zinbanti."

When she goes upstairs to dress, he counts the Oreos in the stack: nineteen of them. He steals the top two and puts them in his pocket. They will probably crumble, he thinks. There are grounds in the coffee she has made for him.

The road to the airport seems particularly light and barren of traffic, like the road in the country he saw from the helicopter in the dream. It is less than an hour's drive from Boulder to Denver. Lisa is wearing a dark skirt—linen, he thinks—and high heels. There is a nick in one of the wooden heels. She is smoking; the interior of the Datsun pickup is now slightly cloudy. He has stationed a small plastic palm tree, with a curved stem and an umbrella of green leaves, on the dashboard. He stole it from a restaurant in Mexico; in the restaurant Lisa had eaten two bowls of green chili and rested her bare foot gently on his knee.

"Christ, this is an ungodly hour," Alfred says.

"This is a godly hour," she says. "It's called dawn."

"Why did you get all dressed up for Zinbanti?" he asks. "No one has seen you in anything except Levi's and that Olive Oyl T-shirt for nearly a month."

"I like that T-shirt," she says. "It helps me think."

"Great," he says. "You could probably finish your book if you spent a month in Disneyland."

She bites her lower lip. She hates for him to mention her book, which—as far as he knows—is about domestic architecture in women's literature. She is strict with herself, and writes each afternoon; she also rations cigarettes like someone during a war. He stole the cigarettes because they reminded him of the feral, slightly ashen taste of her mouth when he kissed her. He once found an earring of hers in one of his pants cuffs—a small, frail gold stud— and he thought for a time of having his own ear pierced, but he did not know whether it was the left one or the right one that meant you were gay. He could not risk the confusion.

Now she is staring straight ahead. The horizon is smoky; only the highway is clear. On either side, the land is flat. A single crane, marooned on an abrupt rise of gray earth, strikes him with its air of desolation and its neat, crooked, mechanical elegance. It seems to him as rigid with apprehension as a giraffe that has caught the scent of lions.

"Machines have personalities," he says.

She laughs.

"No, they do. Look at you and your coffeepot."

"A coffeepot isn't a machine."

"You're upset because of what I said about Disneyland."

"No," she says.

"You are."

"Don't look so despairing," she says. "Just because we don't sleep together the first time my husband goes to camp in an orchard."

"I'm not despairing."

"Yes you are," she says. "You are *visibly* despairing."

In the airport terminal, since they are early, he buys two cups of coffee. "They have the bitterest coffee in the world," he says. "Right here in the Denver airport."

"Why?" she says.

"It's a mystery," he says.

She looks at him, puzzled. She is holding the Styrofoam cup against her lower lip. "It smells all right," she says.

The cup is patterned with small leaves, perfect and vivid green against the white Styrofoam. He has never seen leaves like that anywhere before. They are like willow leaves, extremely thin, with one central vein. He is amazed. "Look at that," he says. He holds his cup up for her to see: it is the ordinary kind, with a simple brown geometric pattern. "These came out of the same machine," he says. "One right after the other."

"They probably just ran out of your kind," she says.

"I love your mouth when you drink," he says.

She smiles, revealing the gap between her two front teeth.

"Great," he says. "That's the first time you've smiled all morning."

She immediately stops smiling.

Metal detectors make Lisa feel shy, he thinks. She goes through ahead of him, making herself as small as possible, brushing her hair away from her forehead with one hand, as if she is about to have her picture taken. Perhaps she thinks that her bones will appear on the oval screen that the fat man is intently watching. Alfred observes her—the nape of her neck, the fit of her jacket over her thin shoulders—as he is shedding things into the small white enamel tray that the fat man's partner pushes toward him: an old class ring, a Coors belt buckle, his wristwatch. He ducks slightly, going through the metal detector's framework, although his head is several inches below the doorway's horizontal beam.

"Obeisance," he says, to no one.

The fat man behind the screen looks up at him, narrowing his eyes.

"We are all hostages to fate," Alfred says.

"Step aside," the fat man says.

Lisa is on the other side. He can see that she is biting her lower lip; they will be late for Zinbanti. Lisa slides a golden bracelet up and down her forearm.

The fat man rummages through Alfred's things. He holds the watch up to the light. Alfred is standing between the fat man and a low, uneven counter of cement blocks. "We regret the inconvenience," the fat man says. "We are renovating the airport. We've had to improvise certain security measures." The fat man's uniform has a curiously handmade quality. Alfred stares at the white shirt, mysteriously unwrinkled, the collar quite fresh. The fat man is wearing a long dark tie. The tie is patterned with small green-eyed tigers.

"We'd be caught a little short-handed if anything really *serious* came up," the fat man's partner says.

"You're not supposed to tell him that," the fat man snaps.

"It's terribly early in the morning, you know," Alfred says. "I may be a little light-headed—"

"You don't look like a man who gets light-headed over nothing," the fat man says.

"It's not over nothing," Alfred says. "It's over a woman, really."

"What woman? That woman over there?"

"Yes," Alfred says.

The three of them stare at Lisa. She looks straight back at them.

"What's that little bulge in your pocket?" the fat man says.

"Oreos," Alfred says.

The fat man's assistant sighs. "Keep it up," he says. "We've got all day."

Alfred empties his pocket. He holds the Oreos forward in the palm of his hand. He can see that Lisa is beginning to assume the wide-eyed, arrogant expression she gets when there is trouble.

"Yes," Alfred says. "She's leaving me. She's already left."

He realizes he has spoken so softly that even the fat man, who is right in front of him, cannot hear.

The fat man's partner, courtly as a magician, hands Alfred his things. He buckles his belt thoughtfully. The partner watches, unblinking. He is wearing a tie that is patterned all over with tiny gazelles. "Yes," he says. "We've had to improvise here. We're on our own."

"You told him that before," the fat man says.

Lisa takes Alfred by the arm. "That was very odd," she says. "You were there for nearly fifteen minutes. What the hell did they ask you about?"

"It wasn't fifteen minutes," Alfred says.

"It seemed like half an hour," she says. "What did you do, say something smart-assed to tick them off like that?"

She is walking quite fast. Strands of her hair have fallen down the nape of her neck. The gold bracelet looks too big for her, as if she had borrowed it from a much stouter woman. He has never seen her wear her hair knotted like that before.

"It was sort of an interrogation," Alfred says.

"*Ha,*" she says. "You think that was an interrogation? Who the hell do you think you are? Those men didn't know you from Adam. We are here to meet Zinbanti. Zinbanti was in prison for eight consecutive years. Beatrice Catron from Smith says that during the course of a lecture he gave in London last summer he pulled up his shirt and the scars were like the stripes of a tiger."

"Dramatic effect," Alfred says. "I'm sure Beatrice was very awed."

"She was. Anyone with eyes to see would be. He didn't do it for dramatic effect. He did it very calmly, quietly, like a man taking off his shoe in a shoe store."

"It's a good way of making a point, I'll admit that," Alfred says.

"Three of those years were in solitary. He ate little beetles off the *walls.*"

"I realize that," Alfred says.

"You can't realize it," she says. "No one who has not been in solitary can realize what it is like."

"What it can do to a man."

She doesn't laugh. She looks at him, tilting her chin, and he could have bitten his tongue. "I've seen photographs of his cell," she says.

"Lisa, everyone's seen those—"

"Zinbanti scratched his working drafts in the plaster. Then he made a sort of paste of saliva and dust and he painted over the walls so that he could go on to the next draft—"

"Lisa," he says. "This is my last offer. Come back to me tonight."

She tilts her head away from him, brushing the strands of hair from her forehead. "I don't know why you keep on, Alfred," she says. They have reached the gate, and she turns to face the wall of windows. He looks to see what she is watching. For a long while he can see only clouds, and then from one of the clouds a tiny point of silver emerges. The silver assumes a shape. It grows steadily larger.

"Long thin scars," Lisa says. "Crossing his spine like the stripes of a tiger." The plane descends as slowly as a leaf in winter air.

Zinbanti comes down the airliner's ramp as if there were some specific question for each stair in the entire flight: Would this one bear his weight? Was this one sabotaged? He carries a briefcase close to his chest. Oddly, the people behind him, who would ordinarily have pressed forward, making small, impatient sounds, wait quietly at the top of the ramp, watching Zinbanti's descent. Zinbanti comes off the flight of stairs with a sudden leap, and crosses the runway swiftly.

"I recognize you from your photographs," he says. "How do you do?" He looks at the two of them curiously. Lisa looks at him. Her eyes are wide. "I haven't slept for days," Zinbanti says. "Not since I left Milan."

"No?" Lisa says. "You couldn't have slept on the plane?"

"I suffer from the curiously neurotic conviction that if I fall asleep on an airplane the pilot of the craft will also, instantly, fall asleep."

"You must find it alarming," Alfred says.

"No," Zinbanti says. "I simply stay extremely wide awake."

His accent is very light, even tentative, and it seems to come and go, like that of a child imitating an actor. He looks at Alfred. Zinbanti's cheekbones are high and arched, and they gleam as if from perspiration. When he takes Alfred's hand Alfred can feel the bones in his fingers, hard and slender. "I admire your work," Zinbanti says. "Especially the long poem, 'The Flaw in the Crystal.' "

"Yes?"

"I have lectured on it," Zinbanti says. "I always hoped that you would be willing to illuminate certain points for me. There was one student at Oxford—a very observant young woman—who asked me a question, after the presentation of the poem, which I found extremely cogent. I could not answer it myself. She believed that there was an essential quality of 'randomness' to the work, an attempt to duplicate a pattern of thought which would belong to the mineral itself. Forgive me, is crystal a mineral? Not exactly, I believe. I believed that the thought patterns of crystal would be quite uniquely *formal,* in fact, rather than fractured."

Alfred gives Zinbanti a long glance that he hopes is shot through with openness and fraternal understanding. "You know how students like that are," he says. "They'll say anything to get your goat."

Zinbanti shakes his head. "I see," he says. "Perhaps we shall speak of this later?"

He takes quick, long-legged strides. Lisa seems to have made herself narrower and fleeter to walk beside him. "You will get a good look at the country," she says. "Between Denver and Boulder—"

"I always like to know something of the lay of the land," Zinbanti says. "I believe that on this continent also you are subject to constant, forceful winds?"

"They come and go," Lisa says. "Sometimes it's windy, and other times it's not windy. We can drive into the mountains if you'd like. Perhaps this weekend, as soon as you are free."

Lisa's eyes are wide; she is walking swiftly. Her long legs, in dark stockings, seem extraordinarily fine. Perhaps it is the heels, Alfred thinks. She has never taken those nimble, angular strides before; even if it is Zinbanti's fault, Alfred admires the invention. They pass through the aisle near the metal detector, Zinbanti moving a little ahead. The fat man looks up from his screen as they pass. He looks hard at Alfred. His left eye screws shut in a wink. Alfred is startled; he stops in his tracks, staring into the fat man's clear gray eye. He shrugs, and begins to walk even faster. Zinbanti and Lisa are several yards down the corridor ahead of him. Lisa is talking rapidly. Zinbanti inclines his head gracefully, listening to her. She smiles up at him. Alfred begins to run. Zinbanti's cheekbone is only inches above her slightly open mouth. In the lobe of his ear is a slender golden ring.

KEATS

We live on the money from a movie that never got made. Dennis's memories of L.A.—palm trees like enormous decaying twigs; the liquid sapphire of swimming pools; hamburgers eaten in the cushioned depths of a producer's Cadillac—have narrowed, I think, throughout three years of wistful frugality. It was all right, he told me once, while he was still a bachelor.

"What are you now?" I asked.

"I mean," he said, "while I was still living alone."

His script was about a feral child. Oddly, that year there was another film made about a feral child; it got excellent reviews. "It looks as if we've been beaten to the punch," his producer told him, the night of the hamburgers. He was stroking the tomcat that went with him everywhere, in the Cadillac. "No one leaves L.A. with their illusions intact," he said. The cat licked the lid of the Styrofoam hamburger box until it was quite clean. There was an unhealed cut, the depth of a dime, in his left ear.

Still, with the money he'd made, Dennis bought this house with its steep roof and shadowed stairways; from a narrow window at one end of the attic you can see part of the Golden Gate Bridge. More exactly, you can see a single fawn-colored upright, and, rarely, an arc of shining cable. In the back of the house there is a porch with wide panels of rusting screens. Some of the screens are torn, and swallows fly in and out. We are lucky to have this house, Dennis says, because it is impossible to buy in this neighborhood anymore. It was once a banker's summer house—the downstairs rooms are small, the carpentry neat and curiously spare, although one of the bannisters ends in the whorled petals of a rose. The plaster of the ceilings is flawed in places because of a small earthquake a decade ago. Inside the kitchen cupboard is tacked a pamphlet: "Plan Your Earthquake: Or How to Reduce Seismic Hazards." On the dusty shelves you find: a flyswatter so ancient its mesh has a burnished, coppery glint; a plastic Boy Scouts of America flashlight with a cracked lens; several onions with flaking golden skins, threaded with green shoots; nineteen cans of Little Friskies cat food, in various flavors; a tin of Star Olive Oil; a can of Band-Aids; a bottle of Nature's Blend Vitamin C in 1000 mg. tablets, the label showing a remote yellow sun. If these are earthquake preparations, it is hard to decipher Dennis's logic. The vitamin C, at least, seems brave.

Before I came, he lived alone in this house for two years. The first time he left me by myself, I went through each of the empty rooms, staring at the cracks in the plaster, opening the drawers of the dressers. Before he lived alone, he was married. Opening a closet in one of the downstairs bedrooms, I found perhaps fifty pairs of shoes arranged on the floor, each pair placed toe to toe: espadrilles, ballet shoes, slippers, Dr. Scholl's remedial sandals. The shoes were as scrupulously aligned as Muslims facing Mecca; many of them had the sort of spindly heels that suit only very long-legged and beautiful women. I stared at the shoes for a long time. Something, perhaps a mouse, had woven a small nest in the injured fabric of a red Adidas.

*   *   *

Sometimes Dennis tells me that we have to begin to watch our money. "Even if it means cutting some corners," he says. I am not certain which corners he means. It is true that I left my husband for him, and that I am spending a small fortune in long-distance telephone calls to Cheyenne, but that is because of Keats.

"I could tell you were going to leave me," my husband says. "You hated Cheyenne, didn't you? You were never really happy after we left Chicago."

"I didn't hate Cheyenne."

"I knew you'd leave," he says. "I just didn't know it would be so soon."

"It wasn't soon enough to keep us from doing a lot of damage to each other."

"Sometimes you are so transparent, Holly," he says. "You really want me to think this is somehow my fault."

"I don't want you to think it's your fault—"

"I can tell you one thing," he says.

I am eating a slice of Anjou pear at Dennis's kitchen table. The kitchen table is painted black; the black is thick as lacquer, and in places it has chipped away, showing the white paint beneath. One half of the pear is lying in a saucer near my elbow. I cradle the telephone receiver between my shoulder and jaw. "What thing is that?"

"Keats is definitely not negotiable."

A small knife rests against the saucer. Along the blade there is a sliver of wet pear, so thin it is nearly invisible, turning dark along one grainy edge. "John Keats is my dog, too," I whisper.

"You're the one who left him," my husband says. "You've been gone nearly three months now. Why are you whispering?"

"I was the one who took him to get his vaccinations."

"I know you did," he says. "When he was a puppy."

"Not only when he was a puppy," I say. "Without me, Keats

would never have gotten his parvo virus shots in time, this spring."

"Oh," my husband says. "Was it only spring?"

There is a pause. I imagine wind blowing against creaking telephone wires, and the thick blue glass of the insulators on top of the slanting poles along a highway somewhere in Wyoming. "I held Keats," I say. "The needle was nearly as long as my finger. The vet had awkward hands, and he was humming to himself. Keats's ears were folded back against the nape of his neck."

"Never a good sign," he says.

"I put one arm around his chest and held him as hard as I could. His heart was thumping."

"I can barely hear you," my husband says.

I shift the telephone receiver to my other shoulder, turning in the straight-backed wooden chair. Dennis's orange tomcat watches me from the windowsill. I am wearing only a black Danskin swimming suit and one wooden clog. The other wooden clog is in the attic, at the foot of the mattress where Dennis has fallen asleep. I am whispering because Dennis is an insomniac. When I woke this morning, he said, "I could sleep like that when I was twenty-four." "Like what?" I said. He is thirty-eight. "Like a stone," he said. When I laughed, he kissed me, wetting my upper lip. "Would you like to go for espresso, Princess?" I said I would. In the small cafe, he leaned over the rickety table, smoothing the sports pages of the San Francisco *Chronicle,* holding my hand. Sometimes he toyed with the fingers, bending or straightening them. A red-haired waitress poured espresso, black as ink.

"The absence of baseball is boring, but not as painful as I would have thought," he said. "Did you know I was once the Harvard shortstop?"

"No," I said. "You were?"

"Sure," he said.

After we came home from the cafe, I was surprised to find he wanted to make love; after we made love, I was startled when he put one arm across his eyes and fell immediately asleep. In the cafe, he had had two cups of espresso, each with five spoonfuls of sugar. I listened to his breathing, which was light and even, his eyelashes dark against his shadowed cheekbone. "I didn't even know you could catch," I whispered. The planks of the floor creaked below my bare feet. I was afraid to risk even the small wooden *tock* the clog would have made when I fished it from below the fallen quilt.

The tomcat stares. His eyes are large, light green with darker rims. There are ash-colored flecks within the iris. Dennis believes that these flecks correspond to battle wounds.

"You know what I think about California as a place for dogs," my husband says.

"No."

"I think Wyoming is heaven for a dog, compared with California."

"That's not true."

"I know you're in the midst of a Mediterranean fruit fly crisis."

"That's not even here. That's in a different county."

"They're probably raining chemicals on your roof at this very moment," he says. "They like to use helicopters in heavy urban areas, right? Why would I send my dog into a second defoliation?"

"Listen. I can hold the telephone out the window. You can hear for yourself that there are no helicopters." Luke was a photographer in Vietnam; sometimes, when he is startled, his fingers go quickly to his chest, as if to the lens cap of an invisible Nikon. Now he is working for a newspaper in Cheyenne, photographing the waist-high wheat in the fields, various high-school beauty queens, and any deer that wander into the city, dazzled by the neon signs above the bars and the lights of the traffic. The old yellow house he chose for us to live in—we had moved rather hastily from Chicago, so that he could take advantage of the newspaper's offer—was set in the plains, far out in the wheatfields. It was a twenty-minute drive into Cheyenne. Near the house there was a steep bank, formed by the intersection of two irrigation ditches, where I would sit in the cattle-tamped grass with Keats, stroking his back and reading David Mamet plays.

"All I really need is a chance to be with Keats for a while," I say.

"Come home, then, if that's what you need."

"I can't, Luke."

"You can't?"

"I can't. You know I can't."

I close my eyes. The telephone is cool against my cheekbone. Suddenly I realize I am no longer whispering.

"How much does Keats really need?" I say. "There are sticks to throw in California. I can buy him organic dogfood. We even have a lawn."

"I don't want to hear about anything you have."

"It's not very big," I say, thinking this will please him.

"Keats needs room to run," he says.

For the second time, we fall abruptly silent.

"Last night I was scratching Keats on the belly," he says. "We were watching *Casablanca.*"

"You've seen *Casablanca* fifteen times," I say. "You must know it by heart."

"I like the things I know by heart," he says.

The tom shifts his weight so that his toes rest more precisely on the edge of the sill.

"I found something below his rib cage, below that spot which is shaped like Baja," Luke says. "You know the one I mean?" Keats is a Dalmatian, leggy and slender, with a wide forehead and a dry pink curve of tongue that you glimpse between his incisors when he yawns; even the delicately striated roof of his mouth is marked with black spots. The night we brought him home Luke and I gave him a bath. Keats was round-eyed with apprehension, and his slick skin smelled of the straw in the kennel. His claws made a light nicking sound, skidding against the curved porcelain sides of the tub. I held him between my knees while Luke dried him with the hair dryer. He was no larger than a housecat, and shivered violently. All three of us were awkward with one another, until Keats fell asleep with his spine in a beautiful arc, the vertebrae showing clearly, his nose tucked beneath one paw. Luke and I stayed awake for a long while, watching him breathe. Some of his spots were like small islands, others like petals, others the size of nickels, perfectly round.

Now the tomcat lifts one paw, running his tongue down the bone of the foreleg. He never takes his eyes from me.

"I know," I say.

"I found a sort of lump the size of a thimble, and it nearly made my heart stop. I thought Keats had cancer of the stomach. I probed around with my fingers, and it was only a wad of bubblegum stuck in his fur."

The tom gives me a steady, critical stare.

"What is that supposed to prove?" I say.

"It proves I could get very upset if I thought anything was wrong with Keats," Luke says.

"No," I say. "I was talking to a cat."

"A cat?" he says. "There's a cat there?"

"Two cats."

"How can you even talk to me about bringing Keats there?" Luke says. "He would *hate* it."

With one fingernail, I scratch at the black paint of the table. The tom's ears swivel forward at the sound. I wonder silently whether Dennis is still asleep or not.

"Holly," Luke says. "I can't talk anymore right now. A woman is coming to clean the house."

"The house? Why does the house need cleaning?"

"I threw a little party," he says. "The police came. There are ashes in the Oriental rugs."

"The police came?"

"Only two of them," Luke says. "The older one admired Keats tremendously. He threw Keats's old green tennis ball for him, and Keats caught it in the air. They didn't stay for very long. They just asked us to turn down the George Jones." He inhales. "Did you know I started smoking again?"

"Oh, Luke," I say. "You did?"

"I did. My only hope is that the capillaries have more or less rejuvenated by now. It seems unlikely, though. Do you know the odd thing about it, Holly? Now it feels as if I had never quit smoking at all."

"Did you know you can get specially constructed boxes for dogs on certain flights?" I say. "No one even has to touch him."

"When I think about it at all," Luke says, "I imagine him freezing in a dark corner that smells of oil and ozone. I can barely stand that long a flight myself, and I always ask for a window."

"If you feel like that, the vet could give him some sort of gentle tranquilizer."

"You know he doesn't trust vets," Luke says. "I really don't want to put him through that trauma right now."

I shake my head silently, as if Luke could see.

"Parvo virus," he says. "Wasn't that the one where all the dogs died so mysteriously?"

"Yes."

"Mysteriously fast?" he says. In the long-distance silence that follows, I can hear clearly the strike of a match.

I have climbed the long flight of stairs to the attic. The attic is white, with long white exposed beams from which hang crimson and gold and black paper kites. The kites turn slowly on their lengths of string; the struts are of bamboo, the tails of rags. In some of the rags you can still recognize a woman's stocking, or the sleeves or rounded collar of a dress. "Clara cannibalized things," Dennis told me once. His ex-wife's name is Clara Wu; she is tall and Chinese. She left Dennis to live with an architect in Milan. Perhaps fifty of her paintings—nearly identical Oreo cookies, two feet in diameter, on white or indigo backgrounds—are stacked face-forward in the rear of a downstairs closet. The paintings still smell of linen and oil, although in places the canvas is beginning to sag from the light wooden frames. Dennis told me once in a tone of self-reproach that he ought to have known something was going wrong in the marriage: in the last few months they were together, she began painting an arrowroot biscuit a neighbor's child had left on their kitchen counter. Her brushstrokes were small and preoccupied; she complained of the unfamiliar textures of the light. "She was a forager," Dennis said. The architect is rich.

Dennis opens his eyes and stares at me. His second cat—a tortoise-shell female with a certain rueful prowess in turning her round skull against the bone of your ankle, and dark-yellow eyes—observes me from the end of the mattress. Some nights, she tries to sleep on Dennis's chest. Her weight wakes him with a thrust that carries his shoulders from the bed, fists clenched; Dennis's father died of angina, knee-deep in a stream, while panning for gold. One night Dennis showed me the gold his father had sifted from the stream, a packet of fine grains that stuck to the lines in the palm of his hand. "It was a tourist trap in the Sierras," Dennis said. "It cost him fifteen dollars. For what? For this. Not even enough to fill a tooth." He poured the grains back into the plastic bag, and wound the rubber band around it tightly. His father had been with a twenty-four-year-old woman, in the stream.

"You've been talking to him again?" he says. He lifts his hands, palms outward, thumbs touching. From the beginning, he has taken a series of imaginary movies of me—rising from the bathtub, eating a croisssant, inserting my contact lenses.

"He wanted me to know he's keeping Keats."

"He can't tell you that," Dennis says. "He has no right." He sits up in bed, a long-legged man, unshaven.

"Why can't he?" I am willing to be reassured. Suddenly I wish Dennis would put his arms around me. He scratches his chin thoughtfully. "Isn't possession nine-tenths of the law?" I say.

"Not in California," he says. "You ought to know that by now. You ran away from home."

"It's different in Wyoming," I say. "It's very pure. If the dog lives in your house, it's your dog. And it was always Luke's house."

"You couldn't have helped that," Dennis says. "It's difficult for a Chekhovian actress to find work in Wyoming. Stay like that. The light's in your hair. This could be the opening shot, you know? With the credits running down the Matisse poster over your left shoulder."

I shake my head. "You ruined it," he says. "Holly, I can't understand why you two can't work out something a little more realistic. It's not as if there are huge sums of money involved, or dramatic changes of fortune. You left him three months ago. He keeps his Fiat, you get your tatami mats sent through UPS. Almost the only thing you have to agree on is the dog." When I am silent, he kisses my shoulder. "I know it's not exactly a divorce settlement," he says. "More of a pre-divorce contract, but it would prove you had been doing some serious thinking in the right direction."

"I hate the word 'contract.'"

"I can tell," he says. "What else did you talk about?"

"Not very much. Smoking."

"Smoking? I thought neither of you smoked."

"He used to, when we first met. I think he does again, now."

He lifts my wrist. "You're getting bony," he says. "You can't keep living on pears and espresso. Men won't follow you through the streets any longer."

"Is it bony?" I stare at my own wrist, and his dark chin.

"So Keats is the point of the disagreement," Dennis says. "Isn't that so? And he ought to let you have Keats, because Keats is your dog. Isn't that so? You always talk as if Keats is your dog."

"He is," I say. "The distinctions sometimes blur."

"Not unless you let them blur."

"You've only lived with cats. It's different. Cats are much cooler. They don't mix things around, or tamper with the evidence."

He turns his face away and scrapes his jaw along the back of his hand, as if to gauge the extent of his need for a shave. "I suppose you could steal Keats."

"I thought of that," I say. "I could drive up in a disguise and hide him in the pickup. Luke doesn't know you have a pickup. I could smuggle Keats out of Wyoming."

"I'll come with you," Dennis says. "We can be outlaws together." I scratch my knee; he is watching.

"I think there must be fleas," I say.

"In my house?" he says. "There's no way."

"They could come in on the cats."

"I doubt it," he says. I hold my knee up for him to see—the swelling is oval beneath a fan of small blond hairs. In the center there is the innocent tea-colored crystal of a newly formed scab.

Sometimes, out of the corner of my eye, I imagine that I see Keats. It can happen to me anywhere. Once, on University, I thought I saw the quick forward tilt of his shoulders, dodging a Volkswagen van, but it was only a small black child, carrying a flute, who had crossed against the light. Another time, at the kitchen table, I thought I felt the rasp of his paw on my shin; it was Dennis, bending to retrieve a chopstick. When I couldn't eat the rest of my food, he put his arms around me. "What's wrong?" he said softly. "What is it? Don't you like sushi, Princess?"

Dennis and I met in a hallway at the Cinematographer's Festival. Luke had come at the suggestion of his editor, who wished, he said, to explore the possibilities of videotape. Inside the darkened auditorium, they were showing a Charlie Chaplin film I had seen before. When I whispered this to Luke, he only nodded. "I want to stay," he said. "Don't worry, I'll find you." Dennis was in the hallway, leaning against the wall. When he saw me, he lifted his hands and framed an oblong of air. "Those eyes," he said. I was blinking, still making the transition from darkness to fluorescent light; he had caught me off guard.

"What eyes?"

"Your eyes," he said. "You ought to be in *The Cherry Orchard.* Not here. Anywhere but here."

"I've been in *The Cherry Orchard.*"

"Pure intuition," he said. "It goes with my great sense of timing. Would you like to go for quiche? There's a quiche bar down the street, exclusively patronized by gay men wearing chaps."

"I can't," I said. "I'm waiting for someone." I sounded oddly apologetic.

"Would you like a cup of coffee, then? There's a machine down the hall." The coffee was darkly bitter; the cream came from the machine in a sudden, magical dollop. "Do you like San Francisco?" Dennis asked. "Have you walked across the bridge yet?"

"No."

"It's beautiful. You've got to do it," Dennis said. "It makes you believe in the existence of angels."

"Why?"

"I don't know, exactly," he said. "Something about the combination of great height and subtlety, or even the fine line between awe and vertigo. It's an odd bridge. Jim Jones once held a suicide-prevention rally on it, and he ended by saying, 'I can sort of see why people do it.' "

"Can you?"

"Can I what?"

"See why people do it?"

"No," he said. "I just think it's a great bridge." We stood talking, keeping our voices low. When Luke emerged from the auditorium, his hands in his pockets, we were still in the hallway, sitting cross-legged on the floor against a wall. Dennis had pulled a quarter from my ear, touching the lobe lightly, to demonstrate his sleight-of-hand. "Are you dazzled?" he said. Luke was frowning as I stood to leave. Dennis framed the air again. I shook my head abruptly. "You moved," Dennis accused.

"That's nothing new," Luke said. "She always moves. She makes a terrible subject." They stared at each other. Late that night, in the hotel room, Luke whispered against my cheek. "I thought that guy liked you. I thought that you liked *him.*" When I did not answer, he turned away and lay on his back, staring at the ceiling. "We can do Chinatown tomorrow, if you want to," he said.

"I've seen Chinatown," I said.

"You know what?" he said. "I thought that movie would go on forever."

It is Saturday, nearly a week since I talked to Luke; it is raining lightly, and a bamboo rake lies where it has fallen in the misty yard. I stare at it through the kitchen window. Dennis has gone to play basketball, lacing his high-tops with care.

"Holly?" Luke says. He can tell it is me, even before I say anything, by the blur of the static. "Keats and I were just out hunting rabbits. I can barely keep up with him. Did you know I've been smoking nearly two packs a day?"

"Isn't that dangerous?" I say. "How could I have known that?"

"It's been so long since you telephoned," he says. "I thought you would hear a sort of roughening in my voice. I could get to sound like Bogart in *To Have and Have Not,* and it would win you back." He exhales slowly. "We didn't catch any rabbits, you know."

"Oh."

"That's like you, to say 'Oh,' " he says. "I know you'd hate it if Keats ever caught a rabbit."

"I wouldn't hate it. I would just be afraid he'd get bitten."

"He won't get bitten. He did go after a fox late last night, though. We were driving on the highway about an hour north of the house, in the grasslands, and there was a fox crouching over a dead rabbit on the shoulder of the road. You could see the reflection of the headlights in the fox's eyes. Keats took off across a field after him."

"Did he catch him?"

"He didn't really get anywhere near, as far as I could tell," Luke says. "The fox was beautiful, with black catlike feet and big ears. I've never been so close to one before. He took off like a shot."

"Keats came back?"

"After he'd been gone about an hour. There was a full moon, so I just sat on my jacket near the truck and waited for him. When he came back he laid down on the ground and panted until his tongue was dripping. After we got to the house I pulled the burrs from his paws with the tweezers you left in the medicine cabinet. He hated it."

"He always hates it."

"How are you otherwise?" he says. "I have a sore throat."

"You do?"

"I even took an aspirin," he says. "I haven't taken an aspirin in years. It didn't go very well with the tequila."

"What tequila?"

"The tequila I was drinking last night," he says. "While I was waiting for Keats to get back from chasing his fox. You should have seen the moon."

There is something wrong with the engine of Dennis's Toyota. It makes a sound like an old man swallowing, waspish and frail, whenever you go over forty-five. We drive slowly off the highway, onto the shoulder. Dennis polishes the windshield with a rag. "This is the only thing I know how to do with cars," he says. "I've spent my whole adult life learning how to avoid knowing anything about the inside." He taps the hood with his fist. "Be good," he says. Clearly, the sound worries him. His finances are carefully calibrated, the strategies listed on three-by-five index cards. I stole one of the cards one evening, and examined it: a series of sums in Dennis's careful printing, listing the costs of painting the house—materials, labor, time. At the bottom of the card he had written: "It seems unlikely that I will paint the house before 1985, when it will be absolutely necessary." I closed my eyes, still holding the index card. I liked the way the paint was unfurling from the wooden shutters, in curls as tight to the touch as an Airedale's. It made me sad to imagine the fresh white walls of 1985.

At the toll booth, he finds he has forgotten his wallet. I hand him a crumpled dollar; he smooths it against the dashboard before handing it to the woman in the booth. She smiles at him. I imagine that she thinks him unusually handsome, and that she is bored with the Sunday traffic. We cross the San Rafael bridge slowly. The wind cuts across the bridge at an angle; I am afraid that the linen cloth tucked into the wicker picnic basket will be blown away. Below, there are islands and oil freighters in shades of charcoal, their shadows falling depthlessly beside them. "Isn't it a beautiful morning?" Dennis says.

"Very beautiful."

"It was a beautiful idea to come to the beach, wasn't it?"

"I think so," I say. I smile sideways at him.

"We always have beautiful ideas, so far," he says.

His fingers rest lightly on my bare shoulder, except when he is changing gears.

On the beach, there is a blind woman with a Labrador retriever. The dog watches closely as the woman wades forward into the sea until the waves wash against her knees. The dog whines. About a hundred yards away, a man is reading the *Chronicle,* propping it open against one tower of a sand castle. The sand castle is perhaps seven feet wide, with a Chartres-like cathedral, airy towers and flying buttresses. There is a channel of sea water surrounding it; the sports pages fan open across the moat. The man's elbow is quite near a small bridge with splintered Popsicle-stick railings. He has a white belly and broad shoulders. His shadow falls across the page of newsprint sharply, like a cutout.

"There isn't a child in sight," Dennis says. "Is there?"

"No."

"So whose sand castle is it, the man's or the woman's?"

"You could ask him."

"I hate to interrupt any man serious enough to read the *Chronicle*'s sports pages during a baseball strike. Look at the light on the beach. You can see everything. You can see the red hair on that man's knees. Look, you can see the freighters."

The black dog sits, panting, on the shore. The woman has left her shoes near his front paws. "I envy that woman with her dog," I say.

"He's very beautiful, isn't he?" Dennis says. The dog's chest is drying into black spines encrusted with salt. Sometimes he yawns, noisily, anxiously; his tail thumps the sand near her shoes. The woman is now ten yards from shore. She is wearing a black swimming suit. One strap has slid nearly all the way down her shoulder. I can tell that Dennis fears for her: in a moment, her breast will be exposed, and the man at the sand castle isn't even watching.

We are sitting in a hollow between two dunes. My knees are cold, and I have been drinking Pinot Noir. The curves of the dunes are as flawless as white silk. The spread picnic cloth gleams with the sand that has collected in its folds; there are wet plastic spoons, crusts of bread, and the stones of peaches. "Look, Holly," Dennis says. He is lying on his stomach. He traces a series of tracks in the sand with a small twig. "A gull?" he says. "A sandpiper?"

"A sparrow?" I say. "Look how perfect each track is."

"Three toes on each foot," Dennis says. He covers the track gently with the palm of his hand, like a man trapping a moth, and smiles up at me. "I feel so lazy." He lies back and closes his eyes. When I lie down beside him, he takes two of my fingers and presses them against the hollow of his throat, between the tendons. "Hear my heart beating?" he says. "One of the associates of the film company I worked with had a heart attack last month. He was thirty-four. He was on the telephone when it happened. The person on the other end of the line wouldn't take him seriously."

I kiss him. Because he has not shaved, the kiss makes a small rasping sound. I turn my jaw until it rests against his. "Keats has two parallel lines between his eyes," I say. "It gives him this worried look."

"Holly," he says. "I've been hearing about Keats all the time lately. Listen to me: I know you want your dog. I *understand* you want your dog. All right? Please? I'm only human."

There is a light wind, even in this hollow.

He turns, keeping his jaw against mine. His chest is dark, the nipple a puckered, faintly darker oval. The spiral of his inner ear is close to my eyelid; I can see the grains of sand inside. The concavity in the center of his chest rises, falls, rises again. He is asleep. His hand lies near my chin, the fingers splayed; there is sand beneath his fingernails. I feel the steady rise and fall of his rib cage, and press myself closer to his body. The backs of my teeth still taste of Pinot Noir, and there must be sand in my swimming suit, but for a long while I do not move, feeling myself as well hidden as a fox in the curve of a ditch.

"I want to try it one more time," I say. "Please?"

Dennis rests the inside of one wrist along the top of the steering wheel, and steers that way; the highway is straight here. He reaches to touch my hair, running his fingers through it without really looking at me. He sighs. "O.K.," he says. "You're the princess."

I dial the numbers in a lighted booth near the highway. The glass of the booth rattles whenever a truck goes by; there is a heart scratched into the aluminum of the coin slot, but no names are scratched inside the heart. In the distance, over some low brown hills, there is a truck stop, its lights only now coming on. Dennis leans against the Toyota, looking away from the telephone booth.

"Holly?" Luke says. "It's dark. I must have fallen asleep."

"Luke, I wanted to tell you that if you can get Keats onto an airplane for me, I would keep him for two weeks—or a little longer if we could agree on that—and then I'll pay for his flight back to you.

I thought that if we could divide his time equally between California and Wyoming, it would be fair."

"Confusing for Keats," Luke says. "Would he go on like that for the rest of his life, or what?"

"I'm only thinking about the near future," I say. "I only want to see him."

"What time is it?"

"I don't know. About nine o'clock, I think."

"Your time or my time?"

"Yours."

"I had a slight accident," he says.

"You did?" I touch my tongue to the backs of my front teeth. "Luke?"

"It wasn't anything serious," he says. "I was driving into Cheyenne, and I nicked the rear bumper of the car ahead of me. It was a Cadillac. I didn't even think anyone in North America drove Cadillacs anymore, you know. It was like running into a fucking black dinosaur. I fractured the windshield, though, when I hit."

"When you hit?"

"My forehead," he says. "Please don't cry. It's all right. Holly, really, it's all right. I even went and saw a doctor about it."

"You did?"

"The man in the Cadillac drove me to the emergency room in the hospital," he says. "He was concerned about my skull, I think. He kept looking to see whether or not my eyes were dilating, and quoting to me the number of synapses in the brain. He'd been reading Carl Sagan the night before, in some hotel room. I forget what the number was. Actually, he was from California. 'My intuition told me I should never have tried to drive through Wyoming on the way to Cincinnati,' he said. 'But I have always had this nameless longing to see antelope.' That was his word, 'longing.' He felt terrible, even though the whole thing was my fault. His Greenpeace bumper sticker was all smashed up. I told him my wife is in California."

"The doctor in the emergency room said it was all right for you to go home?"

"He did, but he said I should keep kind of quiet for a while," Luke says. "I suppose I didn't think it was going to hit me like this. I was lying down watching a movie, and Keats had his chin on my knee, just sort of watching me. Then I went out like a light. I can't tell how long I've been asleep."

"It's probably about nine o'clock now," I say.

"The movie started about three, I think," he says. "I forget what movie."

My shoulder is against the wall of the booth. Suddenly, I feel the cool pane of glass against my skin, and realize it is dark. The floor of the booth is gritty beneath my clogs. Torn pages flutter in the telephone book on the ledge before me. I close my eyes.

"I feel like a ghost of myself," Luke says.

I think of Keats, the curious arching trot he would adopt whenever he had to navigate through stubble; often, in the wheatfields, the grass was simply over his head.

COMINGS

AND

GOINGS

Two things he knows how to do: read minds and skip stones. He was nearly thirty-four years old before it occurred to him that there might be more than a superficial likeness between these two things.

The problem is, he's leaving me. I have been Cody's lover all this time—I am good at mind-reading improvisations, my cheekbones are high and severe, my legs long enough to look faintly knock-kneed in the obligatory colored tights. Our first days together were spent on the beach, collecting stones. Hold one hand out at arm's length, level with your eyes, the fingers slightly curved. Imagine a stone. The proper stone will fit into the diagonal between the base of your forefinger and the first slight up-curve into the fleshy convexity that is the root of the thumb. The stone should be cool, as full of internal certainty as an egg. A stone is a personal object; you will know it when you see it. Those first few days, wading through the foam behind Cody, the bones in my ankles felt cold and oddly delicate. Behind us the waves fingered our footprints gently, as if

uncertain what to make of them, the long splayed ovals of my toe-
prints, the short impacted oblongs of Cody's heels. When I looked
behind me again they were gone.

Cody's in love with a seamstress in Boulder. I imagine that she lives
in a dark Victorian house with carefully preserved white ginger-
bread above the porch; perhaps it is in the historic zone. She is
blond, with milk-colored knuckles; she has a curious habit of biting
off the ends of stray threads with a sudden foxlike twist of her
throat. Her sheets are patterned with clouds. Above the bed, on
pages of pale green graph paper stolen from an accounting ledger in
the office where she used to work, she has charted her bio-rhythms
for the last five months. The three lines on the chart—body, mind,
and spirit—rise and fall in chiseled synchrony. Things are looking
up: her last lover was bald and played the sitar. He used to perform
cross-legged, in a long mustard-colored robe, on the sidewalk in
front of her house. Each evening when she walked home from work
she would see him—his high forehead gleaming with sweat, the
feathery lines of dirt on the soles of his feet, the small round hat he
had placed on the sidewalk before him, upside down, the corner of a
dollar bill curling above the brim, attentive as a cat's ear. The sight
always mysteriously saddened her. As far as she knew he always
used the same dollar bill, but Boulder proved fruitful for him. His
secret inner pockets thickened and grew musical with coins, the
saffron robe billowing like a picnic blanket weighted down with
stones. When he left he stole her driver's license and a Mickey
Mouse bank she had kept on her dressing table. She drove him to
the bus station at midnight; she didn't know then what he had
packed in his suitcase, and the sides of her nose were streaked and
cold with tears. Mounting the steps of the Greyhound, he turned
and kissed the tips of his fingers, lightly, as if by accident. He
looked like a stranger to her, in the hat.

*   *   *

All of this, and perhaps everything that follows, is as fragile, as much a product of the clumsy wistfulness of the imagination, as the stone you held a moment ago in the palm of your hand. Cody has always complained of my awkwardness; once I spilled a whole hatful of slips of paper into the snow, in an impromptu performance outside a shopping mall in Butte. The questions people had wanted Cody to answer were written inside the slips, the slips carefully folded. Cody still speaks of this when he is upset. "An irretrievable loss," he calls it. In his opening spiel he introduces me as a princess, perhaps to intimate that this is why the dark-haired, knock-kneed woman is valuable; it is not obvious. He says everything to me twice, implying that I do not really understand English—this, though I was born in Washington, D.C. It is true that my mother has a slight accent, handed down from her mother like a recipe for cake, frugal and foreign. The night I was born my mother watched part of an old Clark Gable movie on television while my father packed her things into their ancient chrome-green Ford. There were five flights of stairs from the street to their apartment, and it was raining. My father is a small, nearsighted man who favors— even now—clerkish gold-rimmed glasses which rest heavily on the bridge of his nose. He saw only fragments of the movie: Clark Gable kissing a woman so hard that her blond hair swung backwards, the nape of her neck strangely exposed and impervious; a child running down a dark sidewalk, slipping suddenly into an alley between two buildings. My father has the impression that it was raining in the movie, as well as in the street downstairs.

That was in 1954. My father was working for the government that year, attempting to isolate a toxin found only in a certain species of Mediterranean shellfish. The shellfish were very rare, and the causes of this rarity were mysterious: Had they, as a species, simply ceased to adapt in the wake of intensive harvesting by the fugitive fishing industries that proliferated along the impoverished, sun-struck coast? All of the species' chromosomal attention had been devoted to the engineering of this labyrinthine, delicate toxin; the world of organic chemists had never encountered its like.

The shellfish had no energy left over for aesthetic or architectural improvements, and remained plain gray shells on the brink of extinction. There was, furthermore, the possibility that agents of another country were collecting the shellfish, shipping them back to laboratories in the north in insulated canisters of salt water. For days after their removal from the sea, my father said, the shellfish were still opening and closing according to the rhythm of the tide. He was troubled by these things; he used to keep my mother awake with long accounts of the ethnographic curiosities in the history of the species. The shellfish were first known to have been used by Persian women against the soldiers of Alexander's army. In its effects the toxin is immediate and fatal, even in extremely small amounts; everyone knows that there are certain details about which rapists are likely to remain unwary—what they have for supper afterward, for example. My father was as fond of this toxin, as entranced by the intricacy of its molecular arrangement, as if he, and not the shellfish, had invented it to preserve his own kind.

My parents, when they finally learned of the mind-reader, were disappointed. There had been, for a time, a law student from Harvard who wore a cream-colored jacket and matching linen tie; he spoke rhapsodically of insurance scams. My mother listened intently as he described the interrogation of one old man who had cashed in on his wife's policy while she was still alive. "How could that have worked?" my mother asked. "Aren't there records, inspections, things like that?"

"With a few good forgeries, a little discreet Xeroxing, you can get away with almost anything," the law student said. "It's frightening, how easily it can be done." Under close questioning the old man had broken down, removed his glasses, and wept. "Of course then it was transparent," the law student said. "The way he took off those spectacles, unwinding them from his head, and then you could see his ears standing out on either side of his skull, so soft and naked. The old liar really had magnificent ears."

In the kitchen my mother took me by the elbow. Through the doorway I could see my father, his hands on his knees, nodding in agreement. He looked like someone being interviewed for a part-time job—scrupulously attentive, prematurely willing to be let down easily. The law student glanced toward me, straightened one cuff, and kept talking. My mother nodded toward his jacket approvingly. She has always liked neutral colors, and once complained of the Picasso fish in the Shedd aquarium that they were "garish." Now she held me by the elbow tensely, as if she intended to steer me. Her fingers were surprisingly strong. On the Formica counter there was a tray of water chestnuts, pale as narcissus bulbs, braceleted by strands of bacon. "Did you get these from a magazine?" I asked her. "Darling," my mother said. "He's a very personable young man. Don't you think it's time you learned something about hors d'oeuvres?"

Instead, one evening in the spring, there was Cody. He was working at a small girl's birthday party, and it was nearly dark when I saw him walking out alone across the lawn. He was barefoot, looking at the lighted tables with a kind of pleased expectancy. In his dark tuxedo—the narrow white breast was almost luminous against the dusk—he had the anxious stiff-legged walk a deer would have assumed, emerging suddenly from the woods; his head was thrown back slightly, as if he had been badly startled and had not yet recovered. "Watch this," Celia said. Celia is my friend; it was her idea to have a mind-reader at her daughter's party. Iseult is five, and imperious. She danced across the lawn and threw herself at the mind-reader's knees; he seemed to stumble and catch himself all in one movement.

"Iseult's in love," Celia said. She looked at me. "Can you blame her, once you've seen him?"

"No," I said. My fingers pleated the edge of the white paper tablecloth into a small rose-shape as Iseult led the mind-reader toward us. When he was very near he lifted one heel and set it on the table between us, carefully, as if it were an apple.

"Does either of you know about things like this?" he asked. His heel was bleeding brightly from a small cut. He lifted his foot away before blood could touch the white paper. "I think there's glass in it," he said. In the emergency room he held his ankle with the same self-absorbed expression while the doctor probed the wound. "Good news," the doctor said. "You're going to live." He held out a small curved shard, weightless and vivid as a petal. In the morning, when Cody hopped across the dark hotel room to open the curtains, I was surprised by the grace with which he kept one foot from touching the floor.

My parents came to dinner in the fall, just before Cody left on one of his tours. "We haven't been out of each other's sight for months," he said. "I think being apart will do us some good." My mother had told me over the telephone, quite calmly, that coming to dinner did not constitute an acknowledgment that Cody and I were living together. She knew we were; my father, apparently, did not. I had made mistakes. I had no collander in which to drain the spaghetti. Cody washed the gathered strands in cold water as carefully as if they were a daughter's hair. The apartment was tiny—I had painted one wall of the kitchen Chinese red, and the narrow windows were covered by long bamboo screens. The plates and saucers were dark-blue enamel. My father stepped into the kitchen and stood with his back to the wall, holding a handkerchief to his nose. "Your father has a cold," my mother announced for him. The only thing left for us to do was sit down; the kitchen was too small for four people, standing.

"You've handled everything so beautifully," my mother said. "Is this actually whole wheat spaghetti?" Cody glanced at me uneasily. Above the kitchen table there was a small drawing a friend of mine had done—a thin child with bony, vulnerable-looking knees and wings. No one could think of anything to say. After a time, leaning toward her, Cody offered to read my mother's mind. "Concentrate on the first thing that comes into your mind," he told her. She looked at him. He was wearing an old T-shirt that showed an anatomical drawing of a heart, the separate chambers carefully labeled.

"The first thing that comes into my mind is never *quite* the first thing that comes into my mind," my mother said.

My father cleared his throat softly and began to talk. There had been a perplexing new development in his investigation of bioluminescence, he said. We ate silently for an hour, wineglasses chinking against the blue plates, absorbed in his wistful recital of the inscrutability, the mercurial ploys and subtleties of bioluminescence. It was like listening to a sad, slightly awkward man describe the wrongs a beautiful wife had done. We listened without knowing what bioluminescence was; it turned out to be that thing which makes fireflies light up in the woods.

Cody used to like to rehearse with me. "Imagine you are a small squat woman with a seventeen-room house in the country," he would say. When I closed my eyes I could feel his palm against my forehead, cool and professional. "You are a small squat woman with a seventeen-room house in the country, right?"

"Right."

"Now what do you have in the bedroom?"

"Where in the bedroom? Above the bed?"

"Above the bed."

Against the darkness of my closed eyes I could see the image of an impala's head rising from a polished mahogany plaque. The throat was turned in a slim arc, chin slightly down, the long horns nearly touching the wall. It seemed to be staring obliquely at me; the eyes looked Oriental, and disillusioned.

"Very good," the mind-reader said.

*   *   *

Cody's lover, the seamstress, has a small one-eyed cat that walks across the kitchen table when she is gone. Actually it is not even supposed to be her cat; the morning after the sitar player left she found it shut inside a closet. All night long it had made no sound. It has long whiskers, frail as goldfish fins, and it follows her in and out of rooms, brushing the sides of each doorway luxuriously with its thin shoulders. Once when she went to serve supper to Cody there were pawprints on his plate. The sitar player had named the cat Lotus. Cody calls it Jane. The seamstress never thinks of the cat as having a name at all.

To encourage Cody throughout this period—she thinks of it as an "awkward transition"—the seamstress has taken a different, slightly better-paying job in a sandal factory. The interior of the factory is lunar and brilliantly lit—piles of birch-colored sawdust, yards of silvery aluminum work tables. The seamstress leans above one of the silver counters, punching holes into colored leather. Beside her another woman, supple and stoned, lines the little punched holes with circles of brass. The stoned woman works somewhat faster than the seamstress, which gets them both into trouble. The seamstress punches with a small instrument perfectly designed for punching holes in just that dimension and texture of leather; the sandals that they make are sold in blue boxes inscribed, in darker blue, "For the Natural Foot." Tiny circles of leather collect in a drift by her elbow. Beside her the supple woman leans back, pushes at her sleeves, and extracts an elegant joint, slender as a thermometer. From the corner of her eye the seamstress watches the smoke, coursing along the surface of the silver table as if it were a stream.

The seamstress feels her chakra may very well be higher than Cody's; often now when they make love she has the feeling that he is not quite satisfied. She sews the stars on his new mind-reading robe into the patterns of real constellations; he doesn't recognize them. He has promised to leave me for her, but already there are problems. In bed one night he tells her a long story: once he was driving down a dirt road over the plains to a county fair. In the distance he saw a hemisphere of light rising from the ground, plain as the moon, slowly spinning. He stopped to look at it. All around him there were dark fields, and when he got out of the car he could smell, against the musk of earth and alfalfa, something like distant fire. The hemisphere was gold-veined and brilliant against the otherwise unmarred country night, and as he watched it seemed to brighten, revolving on its hidden axis. He was halfway across one of the fields, running as fast as he could, before he realized it was the Ferris wheel.

Cody and I wade in until the water comes up to our knees. We are not holding hands. Near the edge of the woods behind us there is an abandoned tractor—it seems archaic and irritable, as if it had a sense of purpose that it has only briefly relinquished. The steering wheel has a strange elongate primness, and vines have begun to entangle the skinny tires. The water is clear and cold. I am surprised by the whiteness of my skin, the length of my legs when seen from above; I float in a small, much-patched inner tube, skimming my heels along the surface. Cody swims laps until he is tired, and then climbs out onto the low cement dam at the far end of the swimming hole, parting his wet hair with his fingers, surveying the bottom for a stone. When he finds one he cups it for a moment in both hands, as if to warm it. I float with my back to him. Stones skim along the surface near me, touch, falter, touch down, rise again. Each time a stone touches the water a small circle swells against the stillness. This morning, when he came into the bedroom, I was sitting up, balancing a saucer on my knees, drinking coffee. "I'm all packed," he told me. "You knew this was coming, didn't you?" A little coffee spilled on the bedspread. I traced the stain over and over, as if I were supposed to memorize it. "Don't look so shocked," he said. "Let's go to the swimming hole." The clouds that are reflected in the surface of the swimming hole are motionless, high and distant. It is hard to tell how often a stone will touch the water before it sinks.

*　*　*

What I think about later, sitting in the sand with my arms around my knees, is this: the wind in Butte came around the cars in the parking lot, some of them still with snow on their windshields, and it hit you in the face. Everyone stood with their backs to it, except Cody and me. I was shivering; there was the wind, and there was an argument Cody and I had had, earlier. That day my stockings were green, with a red patch over one of the knees. The people were mostly middle-aged men and women in ragged parkas and scarves, little kids in bulky down jackets and black rubber boots. I held the hat before me carefully while they tucked in their little slips of folded paper. Their knuckles were red from the brief time that they had been exposed, writing. When I tripped and spilled the hat, the slips of paper tilted through the wind into a bank of snow, skimmed its surface, disappearing into puddles, among the feet of people in the crowd. Behind me, Cody cried out. No one in the crowd looked angry, only amazed. They'd never expected their questions to blow away like that.

NATURAL

LAW

Far below the level of my narrowed eyes, in the slanting dusk of Fiat-shadow, the smallest of the three toes on my left foot is caught in the wet grain of a tire tread. I am aware at first only of a distant pricking, faintly nostalgic, the way you feel your sweater tug when the sleeve is caught by a nail. The synapses of my brain have not yet adapted to this doubling—the toe is that of an iguanodon, the nail a crescent of thick translucent plastic fitted into the socket of a sinewy blue-gray toe as curved as a cat's. The bottoms of the toes, as I imagine them, are padded and cool; my heels never quite touch the asphalt of Isaac's Scientific-Upkeep Used Car Lot. Iguanodons were always poised as if about to run—the massive weight of the upper body thrust forward, the incisors exposed in an expression of aggrieved caution. They were herbivores, and their eyes were deep-set ovals within protective sockets of bone; throughout most of their lives, the threats they so anxiously confronted must have been largely imaginary.

"I know it comes hard on the heels of Moon-Rock Reggae," Isaac is saying, so distantly that I can barely hear him, although I cock my huge head ponderously in his direction. The movement threatens to throw me off balance; I brace my dappled thigh against the Fiat. "But I have great expectations for our iguanodon. He's tall enough to be visible from the highway, and even though Whitfield hasn't been working with those stilts very long, he's not bad. Not bad at all."

Gottlinger and Barnaby stare at me, entranced. The Moon-Rock Reggae Event was short-lived. Isaac had improvised a display case, as badly lit as a dimestore aquarium, and inside the case the moon rock rested, a fine-grained pebble as gray as its own shadow. The musicians also proved disappointing. In the men's room each one of them in turn positioned a small, cracked mirror beneath his nostrils, gently furled the five-dollar bill, stared down briefly, inhaled, and said "Ah." When they were done the last one licked the faint dustiness from the surface of the mirror as matter-of-factly as if it were a postage stamp. The "Ah's" did not vary from the "Ah's" they had given for the moon rock, although the drummer—the irises of his eyes were the color of caramel, and his hair rose from his skull in beaded knots—touched the glass wistfully, his fingers only inches from the stone. "Do you get to wish on it?" he said. "Like as if it was a star?" "You're so out of it, man," the lead guitarist said. "It's a rock, not a star. A rock like any of a million rocks in the middle of the road." He gestured at the broad expanse of the showroom windows and the distant ash-colored curve of the highway. The real problem was that neither the moon rock nor the thumping reggae seemed to drive people into a frenzy to buy a used car. Whenever a customer wandered out into the lot Gottlinger and Barnaby fell upon him like hounds. Barnaby is, in fact, rather houndlike, with a long slant of bony jaw and wind-reddened eyes, the corners of his mouth deepened by eternal vigilance. The tweed coat that puckers over his long shoulder blades still smells of the ghosts of a million Lucky Strikes. Gottlinger is handsome, quick, and slender—

he was a private detective for a shopping mall in Albuquerque until the night a jewel thief caught him in the corner of the eye with the corkscrew blade of a Swiss Army knife. "I used to love that shopping mall at night," Gottlinger said once. "It was like a long lovely island at midnight. Even the floorwax had a tropical smell, like lemons or flowers. I was all alone there. The windows of the jewelry stores had those little iron grates that close across them, like something you'd see in a foreign country. That's the quality of criminal we got here in New Mexico, that would try to break into a high-class operation like that with a kid's knife. It just shouldn't happen, in the natural order of things, that a man gets his eye put out with a Swiss Army knife."

"The guy could have been queer," Barnaby said, fishing through the pockets of his tweed coat for a cigarette. He still has a complete repertoire of futile searching gestures, although he quit smoking when his wife left him, two years ago.

"You're trying to be helpful, aren't you, Barnaby?" Gottlinger said. "You're trying to make me feel better by suggesting that I got a glass eye because of some pansy with a Swiss Army knife? Do I look like a man who couldn't hold his own with a fairy?"

"Don't get carried away," Barnaby said. "Nobody calls them pansies anymore." He seemed startled once again by the shape of absence in his pockets; he pulled forth a strand of blue thread and released it into the wind. "Lots of them work out with weights, anyway. They're taking over the Nautilus in their lunch hours. Some of them look in pretty good shape to me—a cup of strawberry Yoplait, a pat of Halston, and they're back to the office. Some of them look pretty strong."

"Could be," Gottlinger said. "Since you're watching so close, you ought to know."

Barnaby turned away and looked out at the highway. A truck labored past with an ill-gauged grinding of gears. The shadowy forms of cattle were visible beyond a rattling screen fencing the bed of the truck. It was a dangerous moment. There have been others: Gottlinger and Barnaby have worked together for fifteen years.

Barnaby could tell that Gottlinger was watching him. He only shrugged, staring out at the highway, and reached into his pocket for a cigarette.

Before the Moon-Rock Reggae Event Isaac's stratagems included the Great Price-Cutting Parachute Party—a dove-colored Triumph suspended thirty feet above the showroom floor beneath a cool shroud of parachute silk, and five free skydiving lessons to anyone who bought a new used car. "New to *you*," Isaac always says, stroking his ragged mustache. In his crumpled dark trousers, a single Band-Aid-colored carnation pinned to his lapel, he seems as forlorn as Charlie Chaplin: Which car could you drive happily into your future? Alone among the four of us, Isaac receives a deluge of Christmas cards each winter. "Merry Christmas or Happy Hanukkah!" he reads aloud, proudly.

"Even with your nose, they can't tell?" Gottlinger says.

"Be quiet for once, Gottlinger," Barnaby says. "You're just jealous."

"We drove the Impala to Texarkana and back," Isaac reads, "and I have to admit it runs as smooth as clockwork except that the little lights on the dashboard don't always light up and of course that isn't your fault."

The Parachute Party, at least, turned out well. An enormous woman in butter-colored Nike running shoes, wearing a Mexican cloak that swept the tiled floor of the showroom, folded the papers for a 1975 Toyota pickup into her fringed leather pouch. "You're a Virgo, aren't you?" she asked Isaac.

"How can you tell?" he said.

"Virgos are fastidious," she said. "They turn out to be the sort of men who live alone with a cat. Those are cat hairs on your knee, aren't they?"

"Copernicus," Isaac said.

"What?"

"Copernicus. That's the name of the cat."

"When you were a little boy you wanted to be an astronomer?"

"Something like that."

"Bull's-eye," Barnaby whispered, reverently.

"No kidding," Gottlinger said. "You think there's anything new on the face of the earth?"

The woman smiled triumphantly at each of the sales representatives as Isaac ushered her through the doorway of his office. We smiled back until the door, a Sierra Club calendar thumbtacked in its plywood, wagged shut. It was hard to imagine the huge woman behind the wheel of a Toyota, which seems to have been designed for the frugal Japanese physique. It was even harder to imagine her—in the lozenge-shaped frame of an airplane's doorway—trusting her body to thin air.

Now Isaac looks inquiringly from Gottlinger to Barnaby. Isaac was once a high school science teacher; he went into used car selling, he says, after he dissected his one thousandth leopard frog, whose spotted legs and miniature maple-leaf feet haunted his dreams. Copernicus had begun to avoid him, too. The cat could smell the traces of formaldehyde, no matter how many times he washed his hands. In a way it was probably a lucky decision; with a small inheritance from his mother, Isaac was able to buy his own lot, and his former students, arriving in shy couples, trusted him to point out the defects in the cars. He keeps a stack of battered *Scientific Americans*, from which he devises his campaign strategies, in a corner of his office.

"Gentlemen," he says. "If I may have your attention for a moment? I realize it is difficult to take your eyes from the noble predicament of Mr. Whitfield."

"He looks sort of bewildered," Barnaby says. "I can't believe a real dinosaur would get that bewildered look in his eyes. He looks like he's afraid of getting hit by a truck."

"I think his toe is caught," Gottlinger says.

"His eyes are as accurate a reconstruction as the evidence will allow," Isaac says coldly. "You see the authenticity in the very arch of that slender iguanodon foot. Imagine the long intrigue of evolutionary forces that gave rise to the shapely iguanodon hock and splendid heel. One metatarsal from that foot, retrieved from the rich Cretaceous muck, is as peculiar and precious as a diamond—"

"Please don't say 'diamond,' " Gottlinger says. "Don't say it lightly, not in front of me."

They never caught the jewel thief from the shopping mall. In his bleakest moments, Gottlinger imagines that he sees the thief, driving by on the highway toward Albuquerque, not even deigning to glance sideways at the hundreds of colored flags rising and falling in the wind above the lot.

"What is it made of?" Barnaby says. He steps backward to get a full-length view; my tail is furled across the asphalt behind me. My jaw feels enormously long. If I tried to smile, a double length of slender bone would thrust forward, exposing ranks of leaf-shaped teeth. The thought makes me suddenly hungry.

"The finest papier-mâché construction," Isaac says. "Not nearly as heavy as it looks, actually. Balsa wood struts throughout the body cavity. A linen finish from throat to belly, to give you that glinting graininess when he moves. That lizardlike crumpling at the back of his head is from strips torn from old pillowcases. The eyes are convex disks of plexiglass. We figured they'd look something like a cat's, you know, with the vertical sliver of pupil."

"How come Whitfield gets to do it?" Barnaby says. "I'm the only one here who's over six feet tall. You could have asked me."

There is an awkward pause. The three of them look across the roofs of the cars at me; they are uncertain whether or not I can hear. I turn my head aloofly in the direction of the highway. My caught toe pinches.

"After his wife left him, I didn't think he ought to try to sell for a while," Isaac says softly. "I thought this would take a little of the weight off his shoulders. And I still think he's the only one who could have handled those stilts. That's a fairly complicated piece of apparatus."

"It's all in the inner ear," Barnaby says. "My mother always said I had an amazing sense of balance. I'd be a natural."

"The only natural you'd be would be a natural fuckwit," Gottlinger says. "If you're so well-balanced, go unhook his toe from beneath the tire of that Fiat before he trips and kills himself."

Barnaby's fingers, prying loose my toe, feel somehow clever. I shiver, and shift my weight to help him. When he releases my toe I back clumsily away from him, my tail skidding up against my hocks. "Hey, slow down," he says. "Take it easy, kid. Jesus, you look menacing." I peer at him warily from first one golden eye and then the other. The banner above the lot, stitched with lettering nearly a foot high, reads, "The Tenacious Cretaceous: Fossil Fuels Strike Back."

For nearly an hour, while everyone else is at lunch, I wander the lot alone, easing my way down the ranks of newly waxed cars. I find myself thinking dreamily of the gleaming leaves of the begonias on top of the filing cabinets in Isaac's office. The stems of the begonias would snap nicely. The leaves would have an aftertaste of cinnamon, prickly and invigorating. Distantly, my stomach rumbles. I rest for a moment against the bumper of a Volvo.

To turn the massive head of the iguanodon to one side, I am forced to begin with a movement low in my back and work upward. My shoulder blades feel as if they are wedged against a low cork ceiling; my skull is cupped within a darkened interior shaped something like a hollowed-out pear, the ovals of the cheeks resting a fraction of an inch above my own. I have not shaved for several days, so mammalian stubble rasps against iguanodon sheen. The light filtered through the plexiglass eyes is tinted yellow, but my eyesight is not so much distorted as rendered velvety. I have trouble distinguishing details in the faces of Gottlinger and Barnaby, but a dandelion growing up through a crack in the asphalt seems as vivid as a sparkler: I can almost smell photosynthesis.

I think of Baryshnikov, alone before the barre in a shadowy, overheated studio somewhere in New York. He was Mia's hero, not mine, but I try to imagine how Baryshnikov would deal with the problem of the iguanodon's oddly prayerful little hands. Would he let the left curve outward naturalistically, while the right rests in the hollow of the chest just above the first pucker of the long belly? Would he tuck them in, the backs of the hands touching like the paws of a sleeping cat? It is warm within this mass of papier-mâché, and sometimes I am aware of a sugary moisture behind my knees or in the hollows of my elbows—glue? It is true that I am learning to dress more lightly, now. "You don't need to wear a tie, Peter," Isaac pointed out, the first time I lifted the heavy iguanodon mask into the air above my shoulders.

"I forgot," I said. I took off my tie.

"You've been a little absent-minded lately," he said.

"I didn't know," I said. "Have I?"

He looked at me narrowly. "Have you been sleeping?"

"I have been," I said, "but it's surprising how many really good things there are on late-night television."

"You hear from Mia?"

"She telephones."

He sighed. "Freud was right," he said. "He hated the telephone." Together we fitted the lengths of the stilts down the long oblongs of the iguanodon's thighs. I thought suddenly of my father, fitting notched stems of bamboo together to form the delicate structure of a kite. Before his first stroke, he liked to work with his hands, and he was always very careful with the bamboo. Sometimes he would take out his pocket knife and shave one of the notches into a slightly deeper slant so that the fit would be more secure. The curls of bamboo amazed me: they were smaller than pencil shavings.

"What do you think of these striations?" Isaac said. He ran one hand along the band of agate color that marks the inside of the iguanodon's leg.

"It's very realistic," I said.

"The patterning was inspired by a leopard frog's," he said. "I felt I owed them some sort of recognition."

"It's very handsome," I said.

"Thank you," he said. "You know, in my fashion, Peter, I am not an unhappy man."

Now I wear the cotton T-shirt that Mia left, the one that says "Sisterhood Is Powerful." It seems safe to wear within the papier-mâché dimensions of the iguanodon. His eyes may be shadowy and somewhat pensive, and there is a skewed expressionless slant to the corners of his mouth, but he is undoubtedly male.

When she left she did not have very much to pack—an antique violin of frail zebra-striped wood, a set of pitch pipes, her Shetland wool leg warmers, some scuffed toe shoes whose knots remained as inviolate as Rubik's Cube, a scrapbook documenting her performance in *Swan Lake.* One critic in the Albuquerque *Tribune* had professed astonishment at her "gorgeously fey young profile, not without an austere element of old-fashioned mystery."

"I don't see why you're leaving on the basis of what one idiot writes in the Albuquerque *Tribune,*" I said. "It's not even a good newspaper." I was sitting cross-legged at the end of the bed, watching her pack.

"It's not only what he wrote," she said. "Although that was a sort of spur. I'm just willing to take my chances. You can't understand that, can you? And what you can't understand, you belittle."

"I don't have to belittle this," I said. "It's pure drivel. You tell me what 'gorgeously fey' means."

"I don't know what it means."

"It probably means he could see your nipples through your Danskin, that's all."

"Everything with you gets down to the lowest common denominator," she said. "I think it means that he liked me. I think it means that the United Airlines ticket to New York cost me $399.95." She folded a black cashmere sweater into her suitcase and stared at it, dissatisfied. She lifted it out and folded it again. It still held something of the ghostly dip of her breasts; she had worn it too many times without dry cleaning. She followed it with a silk slip and a pair of black high heels stuffed protectively with Kleenex.

"That's all you can afford," I said. "Once you get there, you can't even afford to stay." She was planning to room with Gerald's sister-in-law's ex-boyfriend, who had turned out to be gay. Gerald was a dancer in the corps who had trouble with shinsplints. After his sister-in-law had moved out, he had told Mia about the three-room apartment, for which I blamed him bitterly.

"I can always work," she said. "Standing around used car lots in monster suits isn't the only way for someone to make a living. You should know that by now."

"It isn't a monster," I said. "It's a slightly smaller replica of an iguanodon." I had shown her Isaac's blueprints for the stilted, careful architecture of the dinosaur—a mistake.

"Look," she said. "Gerald says that Richard is macrobiotic and listens to Vivaldi a lot. He keeps finches."

"Finches?"

"Pairs of finches. Named after Henry James characters."

"Oh."

"Pe-ter," she said, singing my name the way she always did when she was troubled or angry. She looked at me, and patted a pair of pantyhose into a plastic egg that she tucked safely into a corner of her suitcase. "Did you ever hear of an environment that sounds safer than that—brown rice and songbirds?"

But the last time she telephoned she told me that Gerald's sister-in-law's ex-boyfriend was moving out. "He's going to live with someone who owns a bicycle repair shop," she said. "He gave Richard a beautiful spindly Italian bicycle, except that it already got stolen. All day Wednesday they rode around in a taxi, crying and looking for the bicycle."

"You're staying there alone?" I said.

"No," she said, "not exactly alone." There was a pause that

seemed enormous, the way the moon rock had looked when I pressed my forehead against the glass and stared at it until it appeared to float fractionally above its shadow, like a Magritte boulder, eerie and gray. "I was feeling poor, you know, Peter. I couldn't ask you for money when your commissions have been falling off. New York is a terrible place to feel poor in. It may be the worst place on earth not to have money."

"I can believe that."

"I heard sounds."

"Sounds?"

"Sounds at night. You've shown no sign of coming after me, have you?"

"Is that what I'm supposed to do, come after you? Isn't that a little archaic?"

"Christ," she said. "I thought if I could have counted on anyone to be archaic, it would have been you."

"I thought you wanted to be on your own. I thought that was the point."

"It didn't *have* a point. It was just leaving. I thought that if I really went ahead and left, you would make up your mind to follow. I thought you needed something to jar you out of your rut."

I closed my eyes and imagined her three rooms. Rice-paper shades, she had told me once, and a white wicker bed salvaged from a flea market, with our old quilt—gray, gold, pink, and blue—on it. The stitching in the quilt is thrifty and flawless. One night, before we fell asleep, I asked her the name of the pattern. "Robbing Peter to Pay Paul," she said. When I laughed, she rose on one elbow to kiss me in the dark.

"Pe-ter," she said. "Are you still there?"

"Yes," I said. "I'm here."

"Tell me one thing," she said. "Are you going to trudge around inside papier-mâché until you're thirty?"

It was probably even predictable that, when my mother telephoned, she would echo Mia's question, even though she had never really liked Mia—she called her, secretly, "the little prima donna."

Mia called my mother "the hedgehog," more for her habit of snuffling faintly when she talked than for her spiny gray hair. My mother sighed gently into the telephone, implying the depth of her concern. "Peter, Peter," she said. "Have you considered another line of work?"

"No."

"Darling," she said. "You know you never were very adventurous after your father died. I wish he could be alive to advise you now."

"He might tell me to go on doing just what I'm doing, you know."

"He might, and then again he might not. My instinct is that he would not." We talked for a while longer, so that I could coax her beyond reproaches; her snuffling diminished perceptibly. I gave her Mia's address in New York so that she could mail Mia an interesting recipe for quiche that had been used by Mrs. Arthur Schlesinger. When she hung up, I stared at the telephone for a moment, wondering whether or not to tear it from the wall. I did not. I knew I would regret it within an hour. One of the things I had noticed lately was that there was a much shorter time lag for regret.

It must be late in the afternoon; the shadows of cars are lengthening all across the lot. I swivel my head to stare—I think it is an interrogative stare—down into the face of a child whose eyes have the corner-tipped pale roundness of a lemur's. I feel like brushing the hair from its eyes, but this is impossible. It would require fingertips. The child blinks. A cottony stick, all that is left of a round chocolate sucker, is stuck between her fingers. Sometimes, in her anxious fascination, she lifts the stick and absent-mindedly chews it. Confronted with an iguanodon, chew. Her face is remote: she comes only up to my knee. I nod courteously, feeling my jaw treacherously wobble into a grimace bleak as an alligator's. Startled, she skips away.

I tramp forward a few steps; at a safe distance, she follows. Even her sneeze is tiny and formal. Perhaps she is allergic to papier-mâché, I think hopefully, or to the new-car fragrance that Gottlinger sprays from aerosol cans into the interior of each car, from the cream-colored Datsun 200 to the caramel Mercedes station wagon. Mammals, relying on their ever-skeptical sense of smell, will not buy a car that contains the scent of a previous occupant, however faint or innocuous. I plant one foot in the muddy tire tracks left by a BMW that is being test-driven by an arthritic old television repairman, a friend of Isaac's who was probably drawn to the lot by the beauty of the afternoon and Isaac's own eloquence. They must have driven through the eternal swamp near the far side of the lot, where we occasionally wash cars near a rusted, ancient spigot. Barnaby has also gone, in a VW van whose interior is carpeted in hot-pink shag, driven away by a lean young man in white overalls.

I stalk through the lot, surprised that the child is still following me. I had thought my walk, so laborious, would bore her. She has on child-sized Adidas; the laces are printed with minute red hearts. She bends and scoops a small stone from the asphalt; it tocks against the glistening curve of my belly. She stares. I move—skittishness is impossible—with a sort of wry gentleness in the direction of her parents. If I were Ronald McDonald, they would have noticed me by now, and come to retrieve her. My shadow—cast at least fifty feet across the asphalt in front of me—stretches almost to their feet, like a path I must follow in a dream. They are lucky I am not a predator. The husband wears a fraying T-shirt that says "The Only Safe Fast Breeder Is A Rabbit." The wife keeps her green eyes cast down to the surface of the lot. I can tell from their immobility that Gottlinger is well into his spiel. "A terrific old vehicle, lovely as a boat," he says. "Once you're in this you might as well be in a tank, nothing can touch you. You've got to find a car that intrigues you. It's a relationship like any other, you need that certain something, the chemistry has to take hold. How do you like this wood along the sides, huh? You don't find that anymore. Looks like oak. Rings beneath your knuckles, too." He raps the side of the car; the green-eyed wife jumps. Gottlinger strokes the dented roof of the old Ford station wagon. The green-eyed wife turns and looks through the windshield. There is a small Buddha glued to the dashboard. None of us could get it off, although Barnaby left a nick in the Buddha's knee with his screwdriver. The husband walks all around the station wagon, thoughtfully, with a trace of genuine lust in his eyes, but it is me, the iguanodon, moving toward them one step at a time, who is actually large enough to mount the Ford, if I desired it.

The connection between Gottlinger and the green-eyed wife is charged with erotic awkwardness—no wonder the child strays away. I can barely see her now, because each time I work up the energy to turn my head in her direction she circles beyond the range of my peripheral vision. The mother smiles at her carelessly, and then shakes the hair from her forehead as she looks to Gottlinger. I ought to be lying with Mia where the light is filtered through rice-paper shades; I ought to be whispering against her cheek until the fair hair fans upward with each barely audible word, as if the sentences we needed were composed more of breath and recognition and suspense than of actual sounds. Instead, I wheel in slow motion and start away across the lot. If they are so careless of their young, then I will ignore her also.

I pace the length of a 1958 Chevrolet. Ahead of me, the calm cars glitter in the light. Gottlinger herds the young couple toward the glass front of the showroom, his hand resting authoritatively on the young husband's shoulder. There is already a discouraged jut to the boy's jaw as he glances at his wife. Gottlinger holds the door for them, and they enter shyly. The little girl, perhaps in the boldness springing from the sudden absence of her parents, runs forward and takes my leg in her arm. She holds the curve of the knee, silvery wrinkles against her cheek; she releases it and dances away, laughing. I can see her face clearly—the bony chin, the slightly overlapping petal-shapes of the teeth, the smudge of chocolate in the corner of her thin mouth. The sun that slants across the tinted windshield of the Eldorado ahead of me is prickling at my feet. I am beginning to feel that the principal tension of iguanodon physiology is that, within this enormous body, you are really very frail: the temperature of the blood is at stake with each change in the light.

Below me, the corner-tipped round eyes gleam steadily. She can stare at me until I disappear.

WHY

I LOVE

COUNTRY

MUSIC

Nod is a miner. He has long dark hair and owns probably a hundred different pairs of overalls; he likes to go dancing in cowboy bars. Because he weighs about two hundred pounds and is no taller than I am—about five feet four in my bare feet—the sight of Nod, dancing, has been known to arouse the kind of indignation in the hearts of cowboys that, in New Mexico, can be dangerous to the arouser. Cowboys in slanting hats—not only their Stetsons, in fact, but often their eyes are slanting, and the cigarettes stuck in one corner of their mouths, the ash lighting only with the brief, formal intake of each breath—watch Nod dancing with the slight contemptuous smiles with which they slice off a bull calf's genitals on hot afternoons in July. The genitals themselves are plums buried in soft pouches made of cat's fur; if you are not quick with the small knife the scrotum slides between your fingers, contracting against the calf's ermine-slick black belly, the whites of its eyes almost

85

phosphorescent with fear. The cowboys—with what seems to me an unnecessary lack of tact—often feed the remains to the chickens. Sometimes, living in the desert, you understand the need for an elaborate code of ritual laws; without them, the desert makes you an accomplice in all kind of graceless crimes. They are not even crimes of passion—they are crimes of expediency, small reckonings made in the spur of the moment before the white chickens boil around the rim of the bloody, dented bucket.

"Want to go dancing?" Nod says. It is still early and he has just called. I stare at the picture on the wall by the phone: my ex-usband, standing up to his knees in a stream, holding a trout. In the picture my husband is wearing a dark T-shirt, and the water in the stream is the color of iodine. Only the trout is silver. "That job came through," Nod says. "The one in Texas, you remember? It put me in a bad mood. I want to go sweat out my anguish in a dim-lit bar. And it's Saturday night and you're a lonely woman with love on her mind. Come with me. You've got nothing else to do."

I pause. It is true, I'm not doing anything else: on the television in the other room a long-haired Muppet with a quizzical expression is banging on a black toy piano with a toy hammer. My ex-husband is in Oregon. The trout, when he had opened it, was full of beautiful parallel bones. I was amazed by the transparency of the bones, and the fact that they had been laid down so perfectly inside the fish, lining the silvery gash of its intestines. My husband was pleased that I was taking such an interest in the trout. "This is an art," he said. He showed me the minnow he had found, perfectly whole, inside the belly cavity. The minnow had tiny, astonished eyes. I wanted to put it in water. He refused. He wrapped it in a scrap of newspaper and threw it away. "It was *dead*," he told me. When he finally called me from Oregon, I could hear a woman singing in the background. My husband pretended it was the radio.

Nod waits a moment longer. "Come on," he says. "I already told you I'm in a bad mood. I don't want to wait around on the phone all night."

"Why are you in a bad mood?" I counter. "Most people would be in a good mood if their job had just come through."

"Coal mining always put me in a bad mood," Nod says. "Now get dressed and let's go to the Line Camp. I'll be at your house in twenty minutes."

I hang up the phone and go into the other room to get dressed, pulling on my Calvin Klein jeans while the long-haired Muppet sings "The Circle Song."

The cowboys, leaning against the left-hand wall as you go in, look you over with the barest movement of the eye, the eyelid not even contracting, the pupil dark through the haze of cigarette smoke, the mouth downcurved, the silent shifting of the pelvis against the wall by which one signals a distant quickening of erotic possibility. The band is playing "Whiskey River." My white buck-skin cowboy boots—I painted the roses myself, tracing the petals from a library book—earn me a measure of serious consideration, the row of Levi-shaded pelvises against the wall swiveling slightly (they can swagger standing still, for these are the highest of their art, O men) as I go by, the line of cigarettes flicking like the ears of horses left standing in the rain, movement for the sake of move-ment only. The cowboys stand, smoking, staring out at the dance floor. Everyone who comes in has to pass by them. My hair has been brushed until it gleams, my lips are dark with costly gels. I pay my five dollars. Nod follows me. He pays his five dollars. The man at the card table, collecting the money, has curly sideburns that nearly meet under his chin. He whistles under his breath, so softly I can't tell whether it is "Whiskey River" or something else. He keeps the money in a fishing-tackle box, quarters and dimes in the metal compartments that should have held coiled line, tiny amber flies. The cowboys shift uneasily against the wall. Nod graces them with a funereal sideways miner's glance, the front of his overalls decorated with an iron-on sticker of Mickey Mouse, giving the peace sign. There is one like it on the dashboard of his jeep. Nod is nostalgic for Mickey Mouse cartoons, which I do not remember. Fingers in their jeans, the cowboys watch us like the apostles confronted with the bloody, slender wrists: horror, the shyest crease of admiration, hope.

In Nod's arms I feel, finally, safe: a twig carried by lava, a moth clinging to the horn of a bull buffalo. Nod, you see, thinks I am beautiful—a beautiful woman—and that in itself is an uplifting experience. Nod is, for the most part, oddly successful with women; he has been married twice, both times to women you would think, if not beautiful, at least strikingly good-looking. Nod faltered through his second divorce, eking out his unemployment with food stamps, too depressed to look for work. He listened to Emmylou Harris records day and night in his bare apartment; his second wife had taken everything, even the aloe vera. In the end, Nod says, it was "Defying Gravity" that saved him. He had the sudden revelation that there were always other women, deeper mines. He got dressed for the first time in months and sent a resumé to Peabody Coal. Peabody Coal, Nod claims, knows how to appreciate a man who has a way with plastic explosives. Don't they use dynamite anymore? I asked him. Nod grinned. Dynamite, he said, is the missionary position of industrial explosives; some men won't try anything else. He described the way explosives are placed against a rock face; in the end it often comes down to a matter of intuition, he said. You just *know* where it should go. Now, in the half-dark of the Line Camp dance floor, Nod is not unattractive. I imagine him closing his eyes, counting. (Do they still count?) No matter how many times you have seen it before, Nod says, when you see rock explode it still surprises you.

He holds me tightly, we move around the floor. Night washes the Tesuque valley in cold shadow, the moon rises, the eyes of the men along the wall glint seductively behind their Camels. In the mountains the last snow of the year is falling. On the stage, the harmonica player's left hand flutters irritably, as if he were fanning smoke from his eyes; his mouth puckers and jumps along the perforated silver, anemone flow of sound rising and falling above the whine of the pedal steel. The lead singer is blond and holds the microphone close to her teeth. She is wearing a blue satin shirt, the beaded fringe above the breasts causing her nipples to rise expectantly in dark ovals the size of wedding rings.

"Aren't they fine?" Nod says. He is pleased. He sweeps me around in a tight, stylish circle, my boots barely touching the floor. Around us women dance with their eyes closed, their fingernails curving against plaid or embroidered cowboy shirts, their thoughts—who can have thoughts, in this music?—barely whispered. At the end of the set couples separate from each other slowly. There is a smattering of applause. Everyone's face looks pale and slightly shocked. A couple in a corner near the band's platform continue dancing as if nothing had happened. The woman is several inches taller than the man, who is wearing, above his black bolo tie, a huge turquoise cut in the shape of Texas. The woman gazes straight ahead into the air above the man's slick black hair. It is very quiet. Around us people are moving away, to tables, to the bar against the far wall. Nod takes me by the hand. Someone unplugs the cord of the microphone. The harmonica player is left standing alone in the light, talking to himself. He cleans the spit from his instrument with a white handkerchief so old it is nearly transparent.

In the parking lot Nod lets go of my hand. Around us headlights are coming on like the lamps of a search party—dust rising from white gravel, the sound of many car doors slamming in pairs. Nod turns me around, kissing me. Ahead of us a tall girl in a white skirt patterned with flamingos is walking on pink platform shoes, singing to herself in a voice blurred with fatigue. The skirt blows apart around her thighs; she stumbles. Nod takes her gently by the elbow. The three of us walk together to the end of the parking lot, where there is a black van with the words "Midnight Rider" painted in silver across the doors. The windows are round and seem to be made of black glass; there is a sound of drumming from within. When Nod knocks, a man gets out of the van, taking hold of the tall girl—she is still singing, her head thrown back, her eyes now tightly closed. She seems indifferent to his grasp. The man nods to us; he has a light scar across one corner of his mouth which makes him seem to be smiling ironically. He balances against the van, shifting the weight of the girl against him so that she falls inside. The floor of the interior is covered with a dark red-and-black rug. The girl lies on her side; her voice is muffled by the blond hair that has fallen across her face. The man shuts the door. He looks at us and touches the scar with one finger. "She knows the song," he says, "but not the words."

The cowboys had seen us leave together. There was this, which might have been considered an incident: a blond cowboy with a narrow mustache—it seemed to be longer on one side of his mouth than the other—kissed me on the nape of the neck as I went by him on my way to the bathroom. It was a very fast kiss and his expression never changed. The kiss left a circle of evaporation on my skin, cold as a snowflake. It was, I understood, an experiment. In the other room, far away, the guitarist rasped out a few chords, tightened his strings, rasped again, fell silent. He seemed to be taking a long while tuning his guitar. The lead singer hummed comforting sounds into the microphone: one, two, three, foah—

We stood for a moment, staring at each other. This always happens to me when I am confronted with a cowboy in a shadowed hallway; it has to do with having watched too many Lone Ranger matinees during a long and otherwise uninteresting midwestern adolescence. I thought of those Saturday afternoons, looking at him; I thought of the long white mane foaming against those black gloves, the eyes barely visible behind the mask, the steely composure in the face of evil and uncertainty. I tried for a few moments to summon my own steely composure. The cowboy leaned against the wall, cocking one shoulder jauntily. My steely composure had been abandoned somewhere between the second tequila sunrise and the third, and now it was hopelessly lost. The cowboy stared at me. I hoped that I emanated a kind of cool innocence. I understood that cool innocence ran a poor second to steely composure. His eyes were gray, his fingers in his jeans pockets, knuckles riding the ridge of the hip bone, no wedding ring (good sign). Coors belt buckle (bad sign: cliché). Boots of dark suede with tall slanting heels (good sign). Gray eyes (neutral). Slight smile (very good sign: he is not pressing the issue, neither is he willing just to let it drop). I stood there, thinking about it.

He looked at me. I looked at him. My shoulders—one shoulder only if I am to be utterly truthful—lifted of its own accord. A shrug.

He watched me as I walked away. Out of the corner of my eye I could still see him. He shook his head vaguely, stood and strolled down to the end of the hall, walking with real grace on his tall, scuffed heels. The jukebox was indigo and silver and there was a framed photograph of Loretta Lynn on the wall above it. He stood and looked at Loretta Lynn for a few moments, cocking his head like a bank clerk trying to decipher a blurred check. Loretta Lynn, it was clear, would not have refused him. He eased a quarter from his pocket, pressed several of the numbered buttons, and waited. When nothing happened, he leaned forward and nudged the juke-box suddenly with his hip. I could hear the coin drop from where I stood.

The door to the women's room says "Fillies." Inside there was a fat lady powdering her nose; she watched me from the corner of her eye. Tonight, I thought, everyone is watching everyone from the corners of their eyes. I closed the door and latched it. I could hear the fat woman sigh deeply as she clicked her compact shut.

Nod would have been a diamond miner if there had been any dia-monds in New Mexico: he only missed it by a continent. He could have been in South Africa, supervising the long-fingered black men in the dank caverns, if his father hadn't been a physicist in Los

Alamos. But he was, and Nod regrets it. Diamonds, he says, think of that, coming out of the earth, thinking hard, now that would be *something,* the first human being to touch a *diamond.* Of course they don't look like diamonds right away, but you can tell. In South Africa the men dig hunched over—it is "uneconomic," in the words of the mining companies, to dig away enough earth for the men to stand upright, the traditional vertical posture of *Homo sapiens,* but not, it seems, of miners. So the miners of diamonds remain for years in their position of enforced reverence, on their knees. The depths of the earth are open to them, the glinting, ancient lights buried within are retrieved and sold, only to end up on the fingers of virgins in fraternity house basements.

The night had clouded over, leaving only the moon, which followed us from behind. Nod was driving. The Toyota jeep bucked in second gear over the narrow, stony road. Below us on the left was an abyss filled with the looming, lightning-struck tips of ponderosa pines, wind stroking through the heavy branches until they roared. Occasionally a single branch glittered in the moonlight. I stared down at my boots. I had placed them carefully, toe by toe, out of the way of the gear shift. Now the toes seemed remote, indifferent as the pointed skulls of lizards. I was very tired. "No," Nod said, rubbing a clear space in the mist that covered the windshield. "That light you see over there, *that's* the moon." I looked. It was bright as a flying saucer, cold and white, full of intelligent life.

When we got to the end of the road Nod parked the jeep, pulling out the handbrake. He stood at the entrance to the mine, his hands thrust into the pockets of his overalls, looking down. "This whole mountain is honeycombed with mines," he said. I did not feel reassured. He bent and threw a small stone into the interior. It made a very small chink, like a ring tapped against a mirror. "This is one of the oldest," Nod said. "Look how they cut the wood for those braces. Look at the craftsmanship in those notches. Those fuckers are going to last a thousand years." I looked. I could see nothing except darkness.

"Smell the coal," Nod said.

He went back to the jeep for a light. Nod always carries rare and useful things in his jeep: a bottle of Algerian wine, a blanket, a light. He drove the jeep a few more feet forward so that the headlights glared down into the entrance of the mine; this was so we could find our way out. The light grew hazy only a few feet from the front of the jeep. The jeep itself seemed mystically beautiful—a lost island, an airplane after you have just jumped out.

"Minotaur," I sang out. "Come home. Ally-ally-ox-in-free." Nod laughed. I was more than a little drunk.

"We always said it different," he said. "We always used to say, 'Ally-ally-in-come-free.' " He ran the light down the curved walls. The walls were dark and seemed to have been chiseled; the light barely touched them. We did not go far. "Here," Nod said. He got down on his knees. The earth at the floor of the shaft seemed raw and gemmy, as if it had never quite healed. Nod's shadow swept along the walls. He took off his overalls and stepped away from them lightly. Barefoot, he swung the beam of the flashlight in my direction.

"Nod," I said. "Take the damn light out of my eyes."

"I love you," he said. He turned the light off. I could hear nothing. No sound from Nod. No matches in the pockets of my jeans. I cursed heatedly: the cowboy, Nod, the darkness, the mine, Algerian wine, the full moon, Calvin Klein.

"Find me," he said, out of the darkness.

I wished for a long moment that I was with the cowboy, fucking in the back of his International on an old Mexican blanket smelling of dog hair, between bales of pink-yellow hay.

"Nod," I said. "It's dark, it's cold. I'm tired. Do you want to make love or do you want to fuck around all night?"

(The idea suddenly of his agile two-hundred-pound mass moving naked down the gleam-wet corridors forever and ever.)

I lay down on the blanket. I took off my boots. "Ally-ally-in-come-free," I said. He was very drunk. Suppose he got lost, how would I ever find him? "Ally-ally-come-home-free," I called. The wine bottle tipped cool against my spine. I lifted it, held it against my cheek for the comfort of a solid object in the darkness. "You damn well better get your ass *over* here," I screamed. I waited. If he was anywhere near at all he could hear my crying.

When he came from the darkness he was different: he had small curved horns, yellow tipped with ebony, and his eyes were dark in the centers, ringed all the way around with startled white, his forehead covered with ringlets damp as a rock star's. He stared at me. I stared at him.

For a long while neither of us moved. In the light from the headlights small motes of dust danced around his horns.

"It's a lovely trick, Nod," I said. "How long have you had that thing hidden down here?"

I stood up and pulled down my jeans, tripping slightly in the process. I laid them in the corner of the blanket near my cowboy boots, feeling for the bottle again in the darkness. I held it up for him to see. He stood with his mouth half-open.

"What the hell is the matter with you?" I said. "Haven't you ever seen a naked woman before?"

He took a small step toward me. I undid my shirt, one button at a time. "I want you, O.K.?" I said. "Nod, is that what you wanted me to say? I want you. Come over here, Nod. I want you right now." He came toward me, lowering his head. He was not clumsy. Miners never are, in the dark.

Nod, like all true heroes, left in the morning for Austin. He had written down my address on the side of a carton packed full of old copies of *National Geographic*. His cat, asleep on a pile of dirty overalls in the back of the jeep, opened one eye and regarded me coldly. She was not jealous, Nod said. She just disliked being looked at while she was trying to sleep; anyone would. Nod had on a pair of immaculate white overalls over a striped T-shirt. There was a red ceramic heart pinned to the front of the overalls. He had curled the

Rand McNally Road Atlas into a tube in his left hand, and now he swung it idly, as if it were a baseball bat. His eyes were veiled.

"I'll bring you a diamond," Nod said. "If I find any."

Of course, I thought he was lying.

I told this story to my analyst. Her hair is thick and curly and she sits in a white wicker chair in a sunny front room, listening to God knows what and nodding her head. In one corner of the room there is an old wooden carousel horse. When she first started practicing in her own house, she thought of moving the horse into another room. The horse has faded blue eyes, a pure, vacant stare, small curved ears. Think of the dizzying moments that horse has known—small girls kissing its ears, caramel vomited across its flanks, a distant smell of mountains. Every single one of her clients protested when she moved the horse. She had to bring it back. These are crazy people? I thought. Once, when she thought I could not hear, she made a phone call. The conversation concerned another client. The session she had had with this client must have disturbed her. She whispered into the telephone.

"What is the professional term for someone who eats dirt?" she whispered. She wrote the word down on a small yellow pad.

She must have known it, and forgotten. Here is someone, telling her the story of how, as a child, he had eaten dirt, and here she is, in her white wicker chair, nodding gently, knowing she can't think of the word. When my husband calls from Oregon, the static sounds like sand blowing across glass. Against the static I can make out a baby's crying. He asks how I am. I ask how he is. We are both fine. I count how many months it is that he has been gone; he pretends the baby crying is a Pampers commercial.

A small brown paper box from Austin. The UPS man who handed it to me looked at me queerly because my face was painted. The neighbors' children had been here, and we all painted our faces together. Mine is gorgeous—dark gold, indigo. Silver false eyelashes. The little girl next door has promised to invest her allowance in a box of Fake Nails. The UPS man does not know what to say, handing me his slate. The pencil is attached to the slate by a small beaded chain. His truck—the same color as his uniform—ticks distantly in my driveway.

"Is it going to go off?" I ask.

He pretends not to get it. His name is stitched over his pocket, approximately where his left nipple would be, and below that, his heart. Alan. Alan leaves me the box. He shifts the gears in his truck and drives slowly away.

I open the box.

The earth inside smells dusky, rich. There is no message. I lift it, sifting the dirt between my fingers, sniffing. I even taste a little, hoping it will taste foreign and rare, like imported chocolate. It is only faintly sour. Perhaps a square foot of dirt. It will take me all night, I think. I dig through it softly, trying to feel with the insides of my fingers as well as the tips, the way I imagine a mole feels things with the damp pink skin of its nose, its body cloistered, remote. Certain nuns are not even allowed to see the priest, they receive the sacraments through tiny jeweled windows, in darkness. Only the hand, the whisper, the little piece of bread. "Nod," I whisper. The name goes no farther than the smoke from a match. The dirt feels good, it crusts against my fingers beneath the nails. I rub a small clod against my teeth, like a child toying with an aspirin, letting it dissolve into separate bitter grains. I lift two handfuls and finger the dry clumps, breaking the soft clods apart, watching them fall.

SWANS

Below the blade of the scalpel the leech contracts into a silken black knot. Within the knot there are other, distilled points of darkness. Leeches are hermaphroditic, so this one has, in addition to its sucking disks, several pairs of testes and one pair of ovaries, all within two centimeters of sleek ringed skin. Jake moves the tip of the scalpel along the inside of the vial. The leech unwinds into a feather-shape with translucent edges, seeking some point of purchase on the glass.

"*Glossiphonia complanata,*" Spoon says, over his shoulder. He is already washing his hands in the laboratory sink. "You could hazard a guess about the way they got into the swan's nasal passages."

"You think you know?" Jake says.

"Into the swan's nares while its head is below the surface of the water, feeding among the roots," Spoon says. "There's even a kind of precedent—something like that happened in a loon population in Michigan, once. It must have been about two years ago."

"We used to get leeches around our ankles when we went in wading as kids," Jake says. "We'd sit on the dock and hold cigarettes to each other's skin to make them let go. It even gave me nightmares for a while."

"It looks like these could easily give you nightmares again."

When Jake had made his first incisions into the swan's skull, the bone had yielded an unexpected iridescence, like that of a newly sliced apple, to the probing tip of the knife and, shocked by its beauty, he had strained to remember an elementary definition: *Bone is built of structural units, each composed of a matrix of hard material embedded in which is a network of elastic fibers. These units are arrayed so as to present the greatest resistance in the line of greatest stress.* It had reassured him to think of the bone that way, as a precisely engineered resistance, as he cut downward. The oval of the swan's cheek revealed struts of sinew, a smooth petal of fat. Jake stroked the swan's neck with one gloved finger until all of the feathers lay flat. It was a young male: the throat feathers were rust-colored, signalling an immaturity it would have lost with another winter. Spoon came up behind him and leaned closer, studying the exposed throat and the clamshell-pale rim of the bisected skull. He whistled softly between his teeth. The shadowy, waxen channels of the swan's nasal passages were clotted with leeches, still alive and sliding against each other below the dissecting table light.

"Christ's thorns," Spoon said. "I thought there was something the matter with him, but I didn't think it was anything as bad as this."

"It is pretty bad."

"It almost turns my stomach. No wonder he didn't give me a fight. He had no gleam in his eye at all, and usually these trumpeters come at you like cats, spitting and striking. Now I see. He could barely breathe."

Jake wiped the knife against a wad of cotton already spotted with the swan's blood. "I suppose I ought to take some tissue samples."

"Photographs, too," Spoon said. "You can use my little Pentax. Do you think the other swans on the lake could be infected?"

"I don't know," Jake said. "They've been looking sluggish to me lately. Now it makes me wonder."

He is taller than Spoon; when he looks down at the crown of the older man's head, the scalp shows pale through the thinning dark hair. Spoon and he both wear tortoise-shell spectacles. To Jake they have come to seem the distinguishing characteristic of men who observe wild swans; the trumpeters themselves have a narrow line of black from the corner of the beak to the innermost corner of the eye, which lends the eye that particular shape, almondlike and archaic, and the air of remote self-absorption. The trumpeters are an endangered species. They are probably right to look a little self-absorbed. Jake tilts a bottle of pHisoHex into his palms and lathers to the elbows, the dark hair on the back of his wrists unfurling in the water from the faucet.

"Sluggish isn't good, you know," Spoon says. "Sluggish worries me a lot. This time of spring they ought to be skittish as hell, easily alarmed. Damn, I was getting smug. I thought we were out of the woods with these babies."

"They did seem to be making a comeback."

"Not a fast enough comeback," Spoon says.

Jake feels this as a reproach—they were his swans, and he ought to have protected them against this sort of danger. He thinks of the black masks of the young males, the delicate swagger with which they cross the mudflats near the lake, the relief with which they breast the water once again. He had wanted to chart their rise from extinction, to document migrations through the coded aluminum bands sealed around their bony black legs. There is algae below his thumbnail. He scrubs with a small wooden-backed brush. Lately he has been forgetting things in the lab—his comb with the broken teeth; a chipped teacup from which he drinks his morning coffee; the auburn ends of his cigars, stale and fragrant, resting on the rim of the sink. There is one there now. He thinks, I'm thirty-eight, long past the reasonable time to quit. He dries his hands and lights it.

"I can't believe you did that," Spoon says. "That cigar's been there for days. All your graduate students have refused to touch it."

"It's just getting good."

"You know what you smoke like?" Spoon says. "Like a man who's leaning against the wall in front of the firing squad. You've had this look ever since you fell in love."

"Oh?" Jake says, inhaling. "Have I fallen in love?"

"Does a bear shit in the woods?"

"You tell me," Jake says. "You're the world-renowned naturalist."

"I still don't understand why she left you," Spoon says. "I mean I know that she's married, but she was married in the beginning, too, right?"

"The beginning of what?"

"Why would she all of a sudden pack up and leave like that? You've been half a basket case ever since she left."

"Only half?" Jake says. "That's kind of you."

"I'm serious," Spoon says. "Why did Candace go back to California when the two of you were just beginning to get it together? Weren't you talking about living with each other?"

"Uh-huh. I think we mentioned it."

"So tell me why."

"I can't tell you, Spoon," Jake says. "It's a mystery to me."

When Spoon looks at him, the lenses of his glasses seem sharply crystalline, scoured of depth. One hinge is broken and someone has mended it for Spoon with a bent paper clip. Spoon's head is disproportionately large for his rather thin shoulders and long legs; he acquired his nickname years ago, when a student saw him silhouetted against the glass doors at the far end of a corridor. "Women and men are actually two different species," Spoon says. "I've thought so all along. But I thought that Candace was different. I thought she'd stay the course."

"She's not a horse, Spoon."

"No," he says thoughtfully. "She's not a horse. If I'd have known what was about to happen, I could have talked her out of it."

"Right," Jake says. Spoon—who lives alone in an apartment of fabled disorder, with peeling rose-printed wallpaper and skewed columns of books rising from the floor to the ceiling—is notoriously inept with women.

"Come on, Jake," Spoon says. "Wouldn't it help to talk about it?"

"I don't think so."

"Look at me, Jake. I'm your friend. Spoon. You've known me for years. Don't I look familiar?"

"You look familiar."

"So what can possibly keep her in California, then, Chinese food? Her husband? A Jacuzzi?"

"She hasn't got a Jacuzzi," Jake says. "And even if she did, the doctor told her not to get her cast wet." For a moment he studies the cigar smoke, as if it could tell him the future; instead, he remembers her coltish eagerness on the cross-country skis, the morning three months ago when she broke her leg. She had skiied away from him, down the curving trail, so fast that he had cried out in alarm. When he had found her, the tips of her skis were set at right angles, her left leg twisted below her. It was lucky that they were not far from his Fiat. When they made it to the car, they were both soaking with sweat. He had turned on the heater and Candace, who did not smoke, had lit one of his cigars. "I'm an impressive first date, huh?" she said. There were still crystals of snow in her eyelashes and she looked like a beautiful Groucho Marx, pain emphasizing the single crease between her eyebrows and whitening the skin of her forehead. In the emergency room she had tried to describe her husband's insurance policies to an unsympathetic nurse who made no attempt to reconcile the gangly man in ski clothes with the distant, but apparently provident, husband. Eyelids downcast, the nurse rapidly filled out the form on her clipboard: Her husband's name? Occupation? Religious affiliation, if any? After that, Candace lay back on the white-sheeted examination table and would not look at Jake. In the X-ray her knee was unbearably small and luminous; he felt that she had been cruelly exposed.

After it was over they had gone to his house. With her cast

propped on the sofa, she told him that she lived in a trailer set on cement blocks on a ridge twenty miles from the sea. She had been trying to grow bamboo around the sides of the trailer, but the light on the hillside burned the young shoots, or aphids built their spidery crowns among the new leaves. He suggested screening them with old coffee cans, the lids cut off. She said she hadn't thought of that. Her husband raises goats for milk. She showed him a small scar on the inside of one arm from the time a Nubian doe had butted her into a barbed wire fence. Two years ago they had gone to Africa because her husband had heard of some Nigerian goats that interested him. They were supposed to be marvelous goats, nimble, with silken udders that gave only the very richest milk; instead they were nearly starved, entirely malicious, and pigeon-toed, ticks making smooth buttons in their scraggly fur. They had brought one of the goats home with them anyway, and he had flourished in the gentle California winter, wooing the does, breaking into the grain shed, despoiling what he couldn't eat, as if to make up for all his lean years in Africa. Her husband had named the goat Nixon.

Jake and Candace had talked until after midnight, pleased and cautious, her pristine white cast like a bundled infant that had somehow been confided to their care. Occasionally Jake would pat it in an absent-minded way, and once she asked him to shift it upward for her, and he was surprised at its weight. By their third glass of wine she said she couldn't even feel her toes, they were so cold. In bed it was her turn to cry out; he had knocked her cast with his elbow.

Now Spoon is sorting dissecting instruments into an enamel tray. He has partially veiled the swan's body with a sheet of plastic. One black foot juts stiffly from a corner, and the swan's broad belly seems to have contracted, glossy feathers tightening toward the skin. Spoon regards Jake gravely. "Earth to Professor Brown," he says.

"What?" Jake says. "I'm here."

"Sure," Spoon says. "You haven't missed a trick. Your mind's been on the swans all along." He removes his glasses and rubs them against his stained lab coat, careful not to dislodge the paper clip. "I was in love once, you know," he says. "With a graduate student."

"Ah?" Jake says. He tries hard for the noncommittal shading of the *ah*. He isn't sure he wants to hear this.

"She was even younger than Candace."

"Was she?"

"She was twenty-two. Twenty-two. Do you know how old I was my last birthday? Fifty-four. My heart was like an eel. I could feel it making movements at night, when I was in bed. I went to the doctor. He asked me whether I had taken up anything new, like jogging. I said I had fallen in love, and he laughed. My doctor laughed. And you know what? He was right to laugh. I was a pathetic spectacle. If this old gent in a smock and white sneakers could laugh at me, I'd better pull myself together. She was twenty-two."

"What happened?"

"Ah," Spoon says. It is the *ah* of caged regrets. "Nothing happened."

"How can you say nothing happened? You fell in love with her, didn't you?"

"Yes." Spoon looks down at his hands, still sliding the spectacles against cloth, as if they belonged to a stranger. "That much I did, yes."

"That's not nothing, then."

"It was nothing."

"Maybe it depends on how you define love."

"And maybe," Spoon says, turning away, "it depends on how you define nothing."

They are silent. "I was thinking that T.J. and I ought to go out and trap another one, so that we could check him out," Spoon says. "If the leech population of that lake is really up for some reason, it's going to endanger the rest of those beauties. I want to know how much trouble we're in. It's only intuition, but I've got this feeling that our little male here might not be very different from the others."

"O.K.," Jake says. "Would you come in from the road on the far side of the lake from the blind? That way I've got a better chance of them settling down by late afternoon, and I want to do several hours' observation. If you do get a swan I'll come in early tomorrow morning, before classes, and we'll take a look at him."

"They won't even know what hit them," Spoon says. "And thanks."

"Don't thank me yet," Jake says. "You're the one that's got to try and catch another one."

"True enough. Want to help me carry him into the cold room?"

The aluminum door of the cold room, wheeled heavily open, releases a gust of refrigerated air, and as they lay the swan down one wing glides open of its own accord, the long white feathers slipping into an arc longer than a man's arm, suspended in mid-air. Spoon smooths the wing back against the breast. Jake leans against the wall, considering a coyote with slotted eyes, mouth open in a rather engaging yawn, on top of a file cabinet in the corner. A diamond-back rattlesnake is coiled rigidly on the floor. A lynx, a burr in one tufted ear, lies slackly on its side, the round pads of its large paws dark and burnished-looking. Against the chill scent of ozone and the clinical taint of formaldehyde, Jake seems to smell cleaner things, bone and blood-clotted fur. There is a dainty wound between the coyote's eyes, but it looks slyly alive, as if only patience is needed to get it out of here. Jake touches the cold wall. None of these things seems quite dead; it must be his imagination. In front of him Spoon rises stiffly, his hands on his knees.

"It'll keep," Spoon says, of the swan.

Jake's Adidas are wet. The male swan—larger than the one he dissected that morning with Spoon—is feeding in a grove of reeds perhaps a hundred yards upwind from the observation blind. Feeding is contemplative work, requiring much cocking of the swan's head, an occasional brief preening of a half-uplifted wing. Swans love nothing so much as a 360-degree horizon; they like to know exactly what is coming. Jake squints, trying to fix for himself the swan's perception of the lake—muddy banks, the water shining like rinsed slate, curls of foam linking the bunched stems of the cattails whose heads dip forward each time the wind hits them, loosing tufts of white seeds. Water striders skate across the narrow regions becalmed by fallen logs. The swan's vision is far more complex than this, he knows—divided into above and below, above largely vacant and gray, below alive, cold, and sustaining, with the distilled flash of a perch darting into weeds, the curled glint of a sodden leaf, the general overcast of algae-filtered light. Between these elements the swan floats, feeling the wind on either side of its skull, the current bulging the membranes between its down-treading toes. It is something he often finds himself thinking while he observes the trumpeters—that he would like to be one, if only for an hour. Spoon would say his methodology is flawed.

He rubs the bridge of his nose where the binoculars have begun to pinch. He left the campus immediately after his last class; in the parking lot he flooded the Fiat, trying to start it, and found himself swearing bitterly. The rain had darkened the ruts of the road to the lake, and wetted the tangled grass he had to crawl through to get to the blind. The outside of the blind is really only a pitched roof of wooden shingles, curling loose from their nails and blurred by moss, covered with a layer of weeds and thorny branches, within which is a decaying redwing blackbird's nest, salvaged for camouflage by the duck hunters who built the blind years before the lake was designated a wilderness area. The view of the lake is superb; silently, he offers thanks to the duck hunters' ingenuity. It is a homely blind, companionably rotting and smelling of wet wood. The swans have never suspected his presence. The young swan, its profile sharp against the massed darkness of the reeds, thrusts its head into the water, its brilliant white body, so abruptly decapitated, rocking with the helpless wooden lightness of a buoy. The smooth head shines as it lifts, the long throat extended in swallowing, the wings spread for balance, so that drops of water swell and fall from the tips of the feathers.

Sweet Christ, he thinks, if only she could see this, and the thought seems to strip a dimension of light from the water. He fell in love with her because he could tell her things and she understood; because he had seen in the shade of her hair, its darkness grained with blond, and in the apprehensive cast of her eyelids when Spoon had introduced them at a faculty party, the unexpected answer to a premonition he had been secretly nursing for years. She taught two undergraduate labs and lived, unless her husband was still occasionally sending her money, on a rather paltry scholarship. She was macrobiotic; she often caught colds; she had just turned twenty-eight. Each dent in the blue Volkswagen she drove to school had had significance for him—he counted in them the instances of her forgetfulness, her inability to live alone. The Greenpeace sticker made him grin, and the rusting California plates contained a threat—that she could go as easily as she had come. One evening he had stumbled into the darkening classroom where she was beating two erasers together, raising a sullen yellow cloud of chalk dust. As he watched she began, with weary circular motions, to erase her own spiky handwriting from dusty slate:

$$6 \ CO_2 + 12 \ H_2O = C_6H_{12}O_6 + 6 \ H_2O$$

He resolved not to begin by pointing out her error. When she looked over her shoulder, he was smiling. "God, I'm exhausted," she said. "How do you stand this?"

"I don't know if I do stand it, exactly," he said. "At least not the way you're having to right now. I spend as much time as I can beg, borrow, or steal out in the field."

"Should you do that?" she said. "Are you cheating them of your time?"

"They expect it," he said. "Besides, I'm the most-published younger member of the department, and they let me get away with it."

She looked over her shoulder at him. "You're conceited," she said. "And lucky."

"Am I?"

"Without a doubt," she said. "But you have the sanest look of any man in this university. Maybe because you're not really *of* it."

Much later, with this same insistence on making distinctions, she had asked, "Doesn't it scare you, falling in love with someone who's married?" "No," he had said, and then had been forced to wonder whether or not that was true. What did scare him, what had scared him even before they became lovers, was the haphazardness of their first meeting—the fact that, if she had not arrived that September with the back seat of her Volkswagen piled high with sweaters and ski poles and books, there was nothing in the texture of the universe that could have guaranteed their connection. It was an accident and accidents were nothing to base your life on. He understood how much he had come to rely on empiricism, the way that the physical world offered so tirelessly to repeat itself—the way that water, whenever it froze, made ice.

"It doesn't scare you that I might decide to go back to him?" she said, insisting.

"Nothing about you scares me," he said, and that time he was lying.

Spoon had teased him relentlessly about his new "Candy Apple," while the other faculty members, with rare discretion, had left them pretty much alone. It wasn't easy for Candace, he guessed. Once a fellow graduate student had asked her out and when she told him no, he shrugged and said, "Shtupping Brown takes all your time, I guess." Still, Jake had thought she was curiously free of guilt until the morning, two weeks ago, when he found her packing the Volkswagen. He leaned against the hood, watching the books thump to the floor, the clothes tumbling together as she pitched them in, hobbling to keep her cast from touching the wet asphalt of the parking lot in front of her apartment complex. "How are you going to get there?" he said.

"Molly's driving," she said. "She wanted to go to L.A. to see her folks, so I said she could drive as far as San Francisco and we could split the cost. Her older brother's about to leave for Saudi Arabia or something. He joined the Navy. Isn't that idiotic?"

"This is what you want?" he said.

"No, it isn't what I want," she said. "It's just that I need some time apart from you. It's a mistake for me to try to figure things out when you're right here. When you're so available. Could you hand me that crutch beside you?"

"Don't go."

"Jake?"

"I mean it," he said. "Don't."

"Christ's thorns," she said. She had gotten that from Spoon. "It's not as if I'm going away forever."

"No?"

"This is just some time apart," she said, fitting the crutch below her arm so that her sweater tightened across her small breasts; she looked up at him suddenly. "Can't you see it that way?"

"No, I don't think I can. It's too sudden."

"Don't look so wounded. This is just a way of clearing the air."

"I thought the air was already clear between us." He was looking down at her foot, the dirty edge of the cast above her bare toes. She learned forward, the end of the crutch skidding into a puddle. "It wasn't clear enough for me," she said.

His cold fingers make focussing difficult; he can see his breath. It is true that she telephones often, that she sometimes mentions coming back for the fall semester. He wonders if he is losing his sense of her; just her voice, that quizzical upward inflection with which she says his name, can give him an erection, but he is no longer certain of the color of her eyes. He tires himself, late at night, inventing ways to bring about the crucial conversation. "Do you ever think about getting a divorce?" He would have to say it gently, so gently that she could not possibly misunderstand. He wants to bring this about without, somehow, acquiring the onus of being the one who first raised the issue. Can he simply, plainly, ask her that? He tries to imagine her answer, but it is impossible, like trying to see the swan across the darkening lake.

When he is finally home, in his living room, he crosses the bare pine planks in his wet Adidas and, in the dark, dials her number. He calculates: her time is an hour earlier than his, making it nine o'clock. The telephone rings and rings. He turns on a small desk lamp and sits down. Behind him, on the burnished floor, his footprints show clearly the dark mud of the lakeshore. There is no answer.

In the morning, while it is still dark, he drives to the university. Spoon has left the lights of his car on. Jake reaches inside the old Volvo and flicks them off, noticing an ellipse of swan feathers on the back seat. In the laboratory Spoon is already holding the swan, whose extended foot touches aluminum lightly, the tar-colored skin fanning between the toes. The sink's drain is already tamped with bits of reed and twigs Spoon has washed from him. Spoon works gently, holding the nozzle of the hose close to the back of the swan's skull, rinsing the oval cheeks and the smooth nape. "A beauty, isn't he?" Spoon says. The swan's beak is bound with surgical tape.

"How's he look?" Jake says.

"I think we're in trouble," Spoon says.

"I hate this," Jake says. "He's too beautiful."

"Want to hold him, or do you want to cut?"

The swan arches its neck away from the blade. It stares at Jake's fingers, its pupils dilating. Beneath his hand the beak, from which he is gradually paring the strands of white tape, feels like the wax of a cold candle, faintly greasy. Jake circles the swan, searching for the best angle. Spoon is having trouble holding him. "Got it?" Spoon says.

"Got it."

"I can feel the bones in his wings," Spoon says. "Does his eye seem filmed to you? A little dull?"

"I see what you mean, yes. But he seems pretty fat and sassy."

"His heart's beating like a triphammer."

The swan lunges in Spoon's arms, and Spoon rocks forward neatly, on the balls of his feet, to compensate, moving in a surprisingly graceful way around the table, so that the swan, now off balance, is pushed into the specimen cage. The swan turns, its wings beating furiously, to stare at Spoon. Spoon wipes his hands against the sides of his shabby lab coat. "Caught me off guard," he says. The swan seems to follow him with its eyes. It settles first one wing, and then the other. It does not preen, although the feathers of its nape and breast still bear the impressions of Spoon's fingers. "Ah," Spoon says. "He's sick. I knew it. It's that dullness in his eye. We're going to have to put him down and look for the leeches."

"No," Jake says. "I mean, couldn't we just watch him for a day?"

"No," Spoon says. "We can't. I tell you what, though, I'd like to handle this part all by myself. He's my swan. I brought him in."

"I should be here," Jake says.

"You just stay outside in the corridor and wait awhile, O.K.? We can go for coffee or something later. I'll probably need it by then. We can talk about what to do."

As Jake turns away, Spoon says softly, "You've been had, Buddy." Jake looks at him, but his eyes are closed. He was only talking to the swan.

BRIDGES

Two nights ago my husband caught a flight to Lima on a rickety twin-engine Cessna; one of its wings had been patched with a hammered-out tin can. The lights of the plane, coming on, woke two goats that had been tethered in the eucalyptus scrub at the far end of the field. In the glare the kid nosed its mother urgently and she kicked at it with a bony hind leg before allowing it to nurse. The pilot was an aging ex–stunt man, who cursed imploringly in Spanish, Quechua, English, and German, exactly as if the plane had a hybrid soul—the result of various smuggled and stolen parts—that had to be coaxed into the air with each of its nationalist emotions intact. It was a belief Matthew came to share as the plane rose, rattling and shuddering, from the end of the runway, its wake flattening the eucalyptus scrub. After dawn the ex–stunt man did a few demonstration dives above an azure ridge. Once the plane was righted, Matthew took off his glasses and breathed on the lenses; he polished them against his pants leg. Before putting them on again, he wiped the tears from below his eyes with the back of his hand. If the ex-stunt man had observed this silent weeping, he said nothing, though a lesser man, burdened with problems of his own and uneasy anyway in the presence of an American, could certainly have taken it as a criticism of his flying.

Their rapport ended at the airport in Lima, where Matthew was to catch his connecting flight to Albuquerque. The pilot helped to drag Matthew's battered suitcases across a long field. "What have you got in here?" he grunted. "Stones? I like to think I am a strong man." In the end they shook hands three times, the pilot clasping Matthew's elbow—before and after Matthew paid him and once for luck. The cool of the waiting room came as a relief to Matthew, and he washed his face in the chipped porcelain basin in the men's room, cupping the water in his hands, drying his face on his shirt-sleeve. A small boy, his eyes barely sink-level, begged for change. When Matthew complied, the small boy dragged another, even smaller boy from one of the toilet cubicles. The smaller one was wearing a dress that came down only as far as his buttocks, and what seemed to be a woman's wedding ring, held on his finger by many cleverly wound bits of string and rag. He held out his hand. Matthew gave him a dime, which he examined gravely, turning it over and over. "Do you know Superman?" the first one asked, in Spanish.

"No, I don't," Matthew said.

"Do you know who he is?"

"I know who he is."

"Can he really fly?"

"Yes," Matthew said. "He can really fly." Any other answer would have been met by doubt, or even contempt; still, for a moment, he had considered trying to prove to them that a man cannot fly. But even as he imagined himself reciting the most elementary definitions of gravity, things a child could understand—falling apples, stones dropped from towers—he knew he could not face their disbelief. He stared at his reflection in the small, dark mirror.

Twenty-four hours ago, he had received a telegram about his father's fatal heart attack. He was going home to attend the funeral.

The suitcases he unpacks on our bed contain mostly architectural blueprints, folders of diagrams, documents whose corners are tattered from having been handled so often, so appraisingly, in shabby government offices that smelled of boiled potatoes and the ripe lime after-shave favored by minor officials. Matthew is an architectural engineer. We met seven years ago, while he was still in graduate school; on the walls of the dormitory room where we first made love, he had tacked drawings of housing complexes, shopping malls, fountains, laundromats, and even a cathedral whose copper-bright roof was designed to suffer, year by year, a slow corrosion and darkening. Gradually Matthew's interest focussed on bridges. At the wedding reception one of his professors, holding a slice of wedding cake on a paper plate that sagged under its weight, remarked that in a cutthroat, relentlessly competitive field Matthew's bridges looked somehow spindly, ethereal, as if they were intended for construction on the moon. Nonetheless, he could bring himself to believe there was some future in it, the professor said, and kissed me, almost crushing the paper plate between us; there was frosting in his mustache. The bridge for which Matthew had begun the drawings early last spring was to be anchored in a rain forest, above a river so tranquil that palm branches would sometimes float for miles bearing small, screaming monkeys. Matthew had praised the site to me, its remoteness, roughness, purity. The classically difficult nature of the terrain would be a spur to invention; the mists that rose from the surface of the river would cause the finished bridge to look as if it were floating. Any architect would give his right arm for the chance. "You have your dancing," he said.

"My dancing has never taken me farther away than Albuquerque."

"What if you had a chance to dance with the greatest company in the world? Or what if Twyla Tharp called and wanted you to tour Europe with her? Could anything keep you away?"

"No," I said. "Probably not."

The actual construction of the bridge was fraught with problems from the beginning. Isolation bred defection among the *campesinos,* who yearned for their wives and villages; defection bred sabotage. Headlights and bolts that would take months to replace were stolen from the bulldozer; cranes, the diesel fuel siphoned from their tanks, were mired in ditches of ocher mud. The new son-in-law of a famous general cheated in filling an order for cement: one morning Matthew inventoried a hundred sacks of pale sand.

The trouble is, I think, watching Matthew lift a stained khaki shirt and remove a crushed cigarette from its pocket, that I no longer want to know about his flight, the children begging for change, the problems with the bridge. It is difficult enough that, after six months, he is suddenly here. "Do you know where my dark-gray jacket is?" he says.

"The old one with the baggy pockets?"

"Yes," he says. "Do you think it would be all right for the funeral?"

"It's in the dry cleaner's bag at the very back of the closet."

"This?"

"That's my mother's old mink. The next one."

"I didn't know your mother had given you a mink."

"Her second-best. While you were gone. That one's your jacket."

"One of the buttons is gone."

"Give it to me."

He continues to empty his suitcase. Every shirt, every unmatched sock seems familiar. I lick the thread and hold the needle into the light; he is certainly my husband. At first, when I met him at the airport, I could hardly think of anything to say that did not sound strange or stupid. When I saw his ragged head bow beneath the doorway of the airplane, I sneezed. He looked older than I remembered, more nearsighted; the fine-grained shadow of his beard

gave his face an expression of defeat. I sneezed again, more violently. The woman beside me on the observation deck offered me a
brilliant-pink Kleenex. I took it, sniffling, and thanked her. Below
us a line of men in gray suits slowly crossed the asphalt toward the
terminal. Matthew's scuffed suede jacket, the battered leather bag,
and his anxious, long-legged strides distinguished him from the
others. "Is that your boyfriend?" the woman asked, pointing to
Matthew.

"Husband," I said. "Yes."

"You're wondering how I can tell?" she said. "I'm good at things
like that. For example, whenever I lose one glove I never throw its
mate away. I know I'm going to find it sooner or later. I have an
instinct for those things."

"Oh," I said. "I wish I did."

"My husband's in oil," she said. "What does yours do?"

"Bridges."

"How unusual," she said. "Well, he's very good-looking."

He was inside, looking around for me. I suddenly felt frightened;
if the woman had not been watching me so closely, I might have
turned and run. I jerked my face away from his kiss and sneezed
twice more. He held me very gently, his chin resting on the top of
my head. "Oh, Jill," he said. "My father's dead." It was probably
the first time he had said it aloud.

"I know," I said, into his shoulder.

"The first time I get to smell your hair again, it has to be because
my father's dead."

"I know."

The woman was watching us watery-eyed, as if this were simply
one of the hundreds of small scenes you could observe in airport
waiting rooms—lovers parting, husbands and wives reunited, children admonished to be good. In the dimly lit underground parking
lot where I had left the car, I found that I had lost the keys.
Matthew said nothing. Silently, like an exhausted and slightly inept
thief, he hot-wired the Triumph so that we could go home.

Neither of us wanted to go to bed. Matthew drank hot black

coffee as if it could keep him alert. His expression as he listened to me was remote and sorrowing. "Have you got a box of cornflakes, by any chance?" he said. "I have a sudden yearning for cornflakes." I found a box, far back on a shelf. "Is Kellogg's O.K.?" I said. "I think these are probably stale—"

"Wonderful," he said. He ate thoughtfully, sometimes pausing to tap his spoon against the side of the blue bowl. "I don't suppose you want to sleep together, do you?"

"No," I said.

He slept on the couch in the living room, using an old sweater of mine for a pillow, crumpling it in the crook of his arm. Quite early, I woke to the sound of his fist hitting against the wall. I padded barefoot down the hallway, but he was fast asleep. The torn T-shirt he was wearing for pajamas was a concession to our newfound strangeness with each other.

"Here," I say. "Your button's all sewed on."

"It doesn't match the others."

"It was as close as I could come. No one's going to notice your buttons, Matthew. They'll just be glad you're finally there."

"You promise?" he says. He tosses an Adidas running shoe from his bag onto the Persian rug, holding out a handful of something reddish and crumbling. "See, this is the mud that did everything it could to keep the bridge from getting built. I used to go running in it every morning to work off my frustrations."

"I didn't know you'd started running."

"For the last few months. It kept me sane."

"Did you need something to keep you sane?"

"I needed you, and you were a long way away."

"You were a long way away," I say. "I was here."

"Right. Here, and planning a little divorce to surprise me."

"It was a separation," I say. "Not a divorce. And it wasn't supposed to surprise you. You knew we were having problems even before you left."

"Before I left," he says, "we were talking about having a baby."

"Talking."

"Ah, well," he says. "Talking is to having a baby what separation is to getting a divorce. It means it might never happen, but then again it might."

About a month ago, I had written him that I wanted a separation. It was a stilted letter that took ten pages of blue-gray airmail paper; the postman frowned as he weighed it on a small scale, bumping the brass weight from notch to notch. Matthew never got the letter. It disappeared, probably into some dusty postal bag balanced on the rump of a mule, perhaps even now wagging its way down the switchbacks of the trail to the half-completed bridge jutting out over the smooth river. "Any terrain that could sabotage a bridge could certainly prevent the delivery of something as small as a letter," he said, defensively. Until last night, Matthew assumed nothing was wrong.

"There's something crucial that you keep forgetting," he says. "We really were close enough to consider having a baby."

"It's not that I forget anything. It's just that there was no sign that you were thinking about coming back. I was beginning to think I was never going to see you again."

"Only a child makes half a year into 'never see you again.' "

"O.K.," I say. "I'm a child." I am sitting cross-legged in a corner of the bedroom, Matthew's jacket still in my lap, my back against the wall. The button that I sewed on is tortoise-shell, the others some sort of metal; my stitches seem strong enough to hold. My suitcase, empty, gapes on the bed beside his own disordered one. He slams his shut, turns, and grabs me by the wrist.

"Not to me," he says. "So get on your feet. Now, are you coming to this funeral or not? Because if you are, you'd better start packing your damn bag."

In this truck stop, just outside Santa Fe, the menus are mimeographed sheets of yellow paper with a jackalope drawn in the upper margin, just above the "Trucker's Special." A jackalope is an imaginary animal: a jackrabbit with skinny haunches and the curved black horns belonging to an antelope.

"Can I help you, honey?" the waitress says. Clearly, she means Matthew, not me. She scrawls his order on a small pad that she holds against the jut of one hipbone. She looks as if she would like to stroke the tangled hair from his forehead, maybe test the skin to see whether he could be running a fever. He looks dirty and expectant, like a child that's gotten lost at the county fair. His glasses rest on the linoleum table, still beaded with water from the rag with which the waitress cleaned it. He wants the Trucker's Special, whole wheat toast if she's got it. A woman who puts up with no nonsense from cooks and cowboys, she is enchanted by this obviously forlorn young husband; she smiles broadly, as if this were a rare request and she could indulge him. "You're not a hippie, are you?" she says. "Wanting this whole wheat?"

"Not me," he says. "I'm an American. Though lately I feel like I could be the last of my kind."

"Ain't it the truth?" she says. Her name is embroidered on her uniform, just above her left breast. She taps her pencil on the pad as she looks from him to me. Her eyelids are painted emerald green, although the lashes are sparse and red. I say I will have only coffee.

"It's not so bad, Matthew," I say. "We made sixty miles before breakfast. I think that's making pretty good time."

"If the damned piece-of-crap Triumph can get us the eight hundred miles to Iowa, I'll take back every bad thing I ever said about it." We both look around for wood. "O.K.," he says, leaning toward the windowsill. "You tell me. Is this wood or Formica?"

"Wood, I think." We knock. The sound is hollow.

"My God," he says. "If you could only build bridges like that. Put them together like Tinkertoys."

"I thought that's what you did."

He laughs. The waitress puts his coffee down in front of him; he lifts the cup and laughs again. "That's one set of Tinkertoys I never want to play with again."

"Why?" I say. "Can you abandon it?"

"There'd be a list of architects a mile long waiting to take over for me if I left."

"Would you really do that, though? Really leave it?"

"I was beginning to think it was costing me something to stay there, that there was some kind of hidden equation. You know—for every day I stayed there I was secretly losing two days of my life. I could almost feel my life being pared away at the far end. The funny thing is that it wasn't my life, it was my father's."

"You don't really believe this."

"I'm just trying to explain the feeling to you," he says. "Maybe living down there you get more superstitious. In the beginning I loved it there. I was at home. I never wanted it to end." He sips his coffee. "You know, for the ancient Incans the construction of a bridge was an act of reverence. Strands of grass knotted to swing across a chasm, yet steady enough to support a train of llamas bearing tribute, linking outposts to villages, villages to the emperor's city. In the mountains not far from where we were working, you could still come across those bridges. The villages have a ritual obligation to reweave them each year, strand by strand."

He lifts his glasses from the table and peers through them. I hand him a paper napkin. "That's what it was like at first," he says. "That's what I kept trying to hold on to, when it got bad."

"We'd better go," I say. "Before Loreen falls in love with you."

"I don't know anyone named Loreen."

"You do now, honey," she says, and expertly fills his coffee cup.

In Nebraska, early in the evening, it begins to rain. Matthew says he is still wide awake; as soon as we change places, he falls asleep with his forehead against the window. I look for something to put between his forehead and the glass, but all I can find is a stray glove, which seems inadequate. The Triumph is hard to handle on the wet highway. I think of the ice you are always warned exists on bridges, and drive slowly, changing the radio dial from one country-music station to another. I drink bitter coffee from the thermos, tipping it into the cup carefully. Asleep, he seems familiar and vulnerable; I'm something of an expert on vulnerability. When I was seven, my father spent one summer shadow-boxing instead of looking for work, as my mother expected him to. He would sleep late, and carry the wobbly lamp into a corner of the living room, tilting its paper shade so that his shadow fell forward against the wall. The shadow was long-legged and elegant; my father sparred with it in his pajama bottoms, backing and dancing, whistling between his teeth. Sometimes he narrated the fight: he was himself, the referee, a crowd whose thirst for blood soared to the echoing rafters.

Often, when my mother wasn't there, he would do a boxer's exercise—clearing the floor, he would lie flat on his back on the nicked wood before arching suddenly upward, only the back of his skull and his heels taking the weight of his body, and roll from one end of the room to the other. It was a matter of honor that nothing except his heels and head touch the floor. When he reached the far wall, he leaped to his feet with a shout and looked to me for admiration. By the end of summer, my cheers sounded thin; I pretended I was hoarse. I sucked a cherry cough drop and applauded wildly.

He was supposed to watch us in the afternoons, because my mother was doing a play with a repertory company downtown. In the evening, she would sit at the kitchen table, smoking, and feed my sister deftly with a spoon. She would observe the suppers my father improvised—sliced pears and Cheerios, graham crackers with jam, cold spaghetti left over from the night before. "It's all right if you want to eat junk," she said once, "but you shouldn't feed it to Jill."

"Why not?" my father said. "Did you ever hear of spaghetti hurting a kid?"

"They need to have nourishing things, like bacon and scrambled eggs or something—"

"I didn't have time to get across to the store. You're the one who got home late, remember?"

"Maybe I would be more anxious to get home if you could get a job."

"How am I supposed to find a job when you've always got something lined up, extra rehearsals, Sunday-afternoon matinees—"

"It's only this one play."

"It better be." He took the spoon from my mother and wiggled it in the air in front of my sister's stubbornly closed mouth.

"She just knows when I'm upset, that's all," my mother said.

"Everyone always does," my father said. He handled the spoon expertly, making it circle and drive. My sister's eyes grew rounder. For once I wished what I never wished, that I could be younger. My father made fitful machine-gun noises, throwing in some hoarse cries from the wounded. "Baby, listen to me. Ah, pretty girl, open wide, I'm an airplane. This is the war-ravaged pilot coming in for a landing."

I pull the Triumph onto the shoulder of the highway near a narrow river. Mud fans from the rear wheels, but the rain seems to have halted. I open the door softly, so that it won't disturb Matthew. In the scattered gravel, among knee-high reeds and clumps of wild iris, I do a series of dancer's warming-up exercises. While Matthew was away I slept twice with another dancer, a teacher of mine; it hadn't been important to either of us, and I thought of it as a rather tender and unsuccessful experiment, commonplace. Nothing to tell Matthew about. In the clear air, swallows are hunting, skimming so low above the river that they nearly touch its surface. One swallow, at the lowest point in its downward arc, catches a yellow moth and bears it away. The moth's wings jut from its beak, silken and crooked, like a bow tie tied by a drunk.

* * *

I wake Matthew hours later, in Iowa. He rubs his eyes. In front of his parents' house we make a crouching run from the car across a broad lawn on which a plaster deer guards a row of rusting croquet wickets. Matthew's mother comes to the door in a long satin bathrobe and furred slippers. The slippers have eyes and antennae—a joke, given to her by Matthew two Christmases ago. "You made good time," she says.

"The rain slowed us down," Matthew says. He takes her into his arms. Their hair, I see, is the same light brown, although his is damp from the rain, drying in ragged curls. Her hands are clasped between his shoulder blades, the long fingers moving idly, as if searching for loose threads in the texture of his sweater. I am still on the front steps; the rain now feels only pleasantly cold. I close my eyes and lift my face into it, and for no reason at all I remember dancing with Matthew's father. His shirtfront had always seemed impossibly white, smelling of detergent and tobacco, its curve too elegant to shelter anything as ordinary as a chest, a rib cage, a faulty heart. He held you a discreet distance away and that distance never altered or diminished. No matter whether the instruments of the five-piece band on the tinselled platform wheezed a rumba or a waltz, he cantered in a four-cornered box, geometrically precise. The crook of his arm was inflexible, his eyes focussed on some point in the air behind you; I was always tempted to look over my shoulder. Sometimes I would be drawn into sabotage, exaggerating my vodka-inspired tipsiness in a doomed effort to make him acknowledge, even by so little as a curious downward glance or a brief slackening of his pace, that I was in his arms. We revolved with the cool fixity of two stars in a constellation. When the dance was over he would shepherd me back to Matthew through a crowd of winking middle-aged men.

"Jill's standing in the rain," Matthew's mother says.

"What are you doing?" Matthew says. "It's snowflakes you're supposed to catch on your tongue, not raindrops."

"Come in right now," she says.

"You look tired," I say.

"I haven't been sleeping."

Matthew shakes his head. "You've got to get some sleep."

"Why?" she says.

"You've just got to, that's all. You're likely to get sick without sleep. Dad would want you to."

"I can't. I can't be alone right now."

"You won't be alone. We'll find something for you and stay with you until it starts to work, all right? We've probably got something in the glove compartment of the car. Do we, Jill?"

"Why would you two kids have something like that?"

"Jill's analyst gives her something very mild. A prescription."

"Jill?" she cries. "Oh, why would a beautiful girl like this need an analyst?" She hugs me. She seems taller; the skin of her cheek is dry. "I've been so worried about the two of you," she whispers. Very softly, as if I were the one to be comforted, she strokes my wet hair. I can feel my heart slow down.

The last time we came to see them, just before Matthew left for South America, we stayed in their house a week. On the last night they gave a dinner party to celebrate Matthew's bridge and the fact that his father had just become three-quarters of a millionaire. "Three-quarters is so much more chic than an entire million," I told Matthew's father. He smiled at me. A dozen points of candle-flame flickered on the width of the table between us. "I'm going to remember you said that, after I make the rest," he said. He was a small man, darker-eyed than Matthew; he had once fought the Japanese on an island whose beaches held caches of rusting land mines and groves of sickly palm trees. On that island, he said, there was a kind of huge crab that could climb spider-fashion up the trunk of a palm and tear coconuts loose. I must have looked doubtful. "Ah, Jill," he said. "How did you ever lose your innocence?" After everyone else had gone, Matthew passed around his Polaroid snapshots—many of them bleached of detail by the rain-forest light—of the bridge site, which was then only a broad reddish road gouged into a slope of charred trunks; they had had to burn the undergrowth away, dousing it first with kerosene in tins that the workers swung indolently, as if they were watering a garden. On the far side of the river you could see the continuation of the gouge, herring-boned by the treads of a bulldozer. Matthew's father put down the snapshots and leaned back in his chair. "There's something I want to tell you kids," he said. "I didn't want to scare you with the news over the telephone. Mother and I have discussed it pretty thoroughly, and we agreed the best way was to be honest, not to try to keep any of the facts from you. It wasn't any use bringing it up before, because you were getting ready to go away, Matthew, and it would only have alarmed you, Jill, to know something Matthew couldn't know."

"Well, Jesus Christ," Matthew said. "What's wrong?"

His father blunted a teardrop of wax that was threading its way down a candlestick. He waited until the wax had dried before shaking the finger gently, the way a cat shakes a wetted paw. About a month before, he explained, he had had a heart attack. He had risen from bed and stumbled down the hallway, falling and catching the back of his head against a corner of the stairwell, where you could still find, if you wanted to look, a nick in the plaster. "I have a hard head," he said. He had been trying to reach the telephone. Matthew's mother did not even wake until the sound of his fall. In her panic, instead of calling an ambulance she had dragged him down the hallway and shoved him into the back seat of the Cadillac, covering his bare feet with a child's jacket she found there. The jacket had one torn sleeve; the soles of his feet were cold. The Cadillac fishtailed through intersections at seventy miles an hour, tires skidding on the pavement, once bucking up over a curb. She had never even noticed whether the lights were red or green.

"So I've got something to be grateful for," he said. "Because if I had been conscious, the ride alone would have killed me." That became the point at which we could safely, softly laugh—my quick laugh, Matthew's hoarser one, and his mother's, reluctant, the laugh of someone who already knows the joke.

In the months that followed he had obeyed his doctor, abandoning drinking and cigarettes, his great loves since the Navy. Matthew's mother continued defiantly to chainsmoke Virginia Slims, drink piña coladas all winter long, and dance with a flirtatious giddiness, pearl-earringed and diamond-fingered, until three in the morning in the Elks club downtown. Although there was no real reason he should not dance, Matthew's father had taken to sitting at their table throughout the evening, and if I am right she must have missed that severe and gentle stare directed over her naked shoulder. The second heart attack was fatal. It took place in the dead of night, like the first, but there was no anguished drive through darkened streets—she had learned her lesson. One of the stretcher-bearers tripped over a croquet wicket and only righted himself at the last moment, putting one hand on the back of the plaster deer. The ambulance, when it left the house, pulled away in silence, only the red and blue lights spinning in turns across the ragged grass.

Now, the morning after we arrived, it is nearly light. I rise on one elbow, denting the mattress between us; Matthew is still asleep. It is a paunchy old mattress, ivory buttons punched into a black-and-white striped covering that smells faintly of mice. Very late last night, it was decided that we should sleep in the attic because the other bedrooms were taken. Matthew's sisters, with their children, had long since gone to bed; funeral preparations had exhausted everyone, and there were unpacked suitcases and a toy robot, two feet tall, on the floor of the bathroom where I washed. We had to drag the mattress up the steep flight of stairs, yanking it from tread to tread. I was a little drunk from the inch of Johnnie Walker Red Matthew's mother had poured into a Flintstones glass for me—drunk enough so that, brushing my teeth in the bathroom, I had turned the robot's key and stared, disappointed, at its arthritic progress across the tile floor. Matthew was slightly drunker. We had dragged the mattress across the warped floorboards to the window; the house below us seemed finally silent. "Want to make love?" he said, when we were sprawled parallel, staring at the slanting ceiling. "What time of month is it?"

"Not a time when I can take chances," I said. "And I hate this ratty mattress."

"You're so spoiled," he said. "What would you have done in Peru?"

"Avoided you."

"You would?" he said. "You really think so?" He turned and cupped my face in his hands. I could feel his wedding ring pressing against my jaw. Only his skin still held the faint edgy scent of his fatigue and grief, and that seemed suddenly remote. Matthew had wedged the window open with a stick; a light wind blew my hair forward, covering his hands. "Would you listen to me?" he said. "If we're lucky, it would have your eyes."

Afterward, he started to say something and stopped. I was lying on my side, not very close to him, stroking his forehead with one hand. He caught my fingers and held them to his mouth as if he were about to kiss them and then forgot. "What is it?" I said.

"I don't know," he said. "I was thinking about that little kid in the john in the airport in Lima. I was wishing I had given him more than a dime."

"That's really what you were thinking?"

"Not all."

"What, then?"

"My father," he said. "Now there are all of these things that keep running through my mind, things I can never talk to him about. There were things I know I should have said."

I moved a little nearer to him on the mattress. He looked at me, but all I could think of was clichés: It was very quick. There couldn't have been any pain.

IN

CONSTANT

FLIGHT

The contact lens floats in the drop of water on the tip of Gregory's finger. As the finger nears his eye, he blinks; the lens, brushed away by his eyelashes, falls. It spins in the bottom of the pool of water in the bathroom sink. Gregory is tall; he stoops slightly to retrieve the lens. He holds it delicately between thumb and forefinger, examining the glass against the light for scratches. This time, he inserts it successfully. The bathroom walls are covered with black-and-white photographs of an eclipse of the sun; the moon is held in a slender ring of white light. Gregory stares into the mirror. Tears stream across the hollow of his unshaven cheek.

"Humphrey Bogart in *The African Queen*," he says. "Do you think I should try those soft lenses?"

I am standing behind Gregory. I can see only a slice of my cheek and forehead in the mirror, and the corner of one eye. The collar of my coat is damp, because I have just come in from the snow. Gregory is naked except for his Levi's. On the top of the toilet tank there is a pair of Natalie's stockings. There is a hole in the toe of one stocking. I am surprised by the cold in the bathroom, the light cloud that forms as Gregory breathes against the mirror. We have been divorced for nearly a year now.

"What happened to that Salvation Army mink of yours?" he says.

"It got stolen."

"I can't believe that. You hardly ever took it off. You looked terrific in it."

"It got stolen from the back of my chair in the Rare Manuscripts room. Listen, Gregory, I can see you're not going to be ready for a while. I left the Volvo running."

"Why don't you go turn it off?"

"It's so hard to start."

"We can walk to the planetarium. Or we can jump-start the Volvo."

"You're terrible at things like that, and it's snowing—"

"It was supposed to snow."

"It's snowing quite hard—"

"It was supposed to snow quite hard. They'll get the snowplows working before we're even out of the planetarium."

"How do you know what the snow was supposed to do?"

"There was this guy in a gray suit on television at five o'clock. He won my trust instantly."

"Oh, fine. Now you listen to the weather. Next thing, you'll be buying stocks."

"It's the middle-aged lust for security, darling. It infects even planetary astronomers." He blinks at his reflection in the mirror and runs the back of his hand across his cheekbone. His eyes are darker than I remember. Perhaps it is only the contacts. He takes the razor from the medicine cabinet, scrutinizes the blade, and lathers his chin. "I think we should have a cup of coffee before we go. It might help calm you down."

"Coffee? Coffee will calm me down?" This takes a moment to sink in. "Who told you I need calming down?"

"It's common knowledge."

"Whose common knowledge?"

"You live in a trailer. Anyone who is still living in a trailer in Boulder near the middle of November needs calming down."

I laugh. Gregory is frowning at his lathered chin in the mirror, the razor in his hand. The channel of his spine, just above the waist of his Levi's, is still beaded with water. Why isn't he cold? Gregory has slender, crooked white toes, like those of a prehistoric horse I saw once in a museum. *Eohippus:* fast and clever, the size of a fox. Sometimes, working at night in his study, he would drop a pencil and absent-mindedly pick it up with his toes. He always worked barefoot, the desk lamp shining on the diagrams of the planets and the pale-green computer printouts.

Gregory shaves quickly, and rinses his hand under the faucet. He makes a face. "I've cut myself," he says. "I haven't done that for months." He blots his chin with a washcloth.

"You shouldn't have shaved it off for Natalie."

"Don't go righteous on me now," he says. "Not when things are so lovely." He takes the Mercurochrome from the back of the cabinet and cautiously squeezes a bead from the medicine dropper onto his chin.

"Gregory, what's lovely?"

"Come here and blow, will you? This stings."

I blow against the cut. It is a narrow cut, no longer than my fingernail. "Turn your face away a little," I say. This near, his skin smells of soap. His beard used to catch in my hair, roughen the skin around my mouth. I used up dozens of Chap Sticks; my teeth always tasted faintly of candle wax. It was a dark beard, with strands of gray, and Gregory kept it trimmed with a pair of small scissors. Now, on his bare skin, the smudge of Mercurochrome widens and dries a faint pink. Gregory puts his arms around my waist.

"That's why the house is such a mess, because of the *Voyager I* flyby," Gregory says. "McFerrin goes to Pasadena with the imaging team, and I end up staying here running the show at the plane-

tarium." We are in the kitchen, drinking coffee. In the bathroom
he held me only for a moment; we looked at each other. Awkwardly, he let me go. The coffee is very hot and slightly bitter.
Gregory has discovered that he is out of sugar. He goes to the
refrigerator, and takes a cup of yogurt from the shelf. "Eat this,"
he says. He hands me a spoon.

"I'm not hungry."

"Would you eat it, please? As a sort of favor to me?"

"You lured me into the house so that you could watch me eat a
cup of strawberry yogurt?"

"You're getting so thin," he says.

"Oboe players look good when they're thin," I tell him. "Unlike,
say, cellists. A cellist needs a certain solidity to appear convincing."

"That's what you lack, Jennifer," he says. "Solidity. You
look like a waif." When I only spoon some yogurt from the cup,
he says, "There are problems with the planetarium. Christ, this
morning someone called me because there weren't enough outlets
in the lobby. They wanted to set up some extra viewing screens.
What am I supposed to do about it? I told McFerrin before he
left—'McFerrin,' I said, 'try to think of me as your old-fashioned,
hard-core Disneyesque researcher, the kind that walks around
with his pants on backward.' He said he had seen a number of
Disney movies and I wasn't in any of them. 'In times of stress,'
he said, 'responsibility falls even on the slender shoulders of our
luminary.'"

"Luminary?"

" 'You're the diplomat,' I told him. 'I'll never be able to handle
this thing with your kind of flair.' 'It's all very straightforward,' he
said. 'Everything you need to know is right there in black-and-
white.' McFerrin now has two ex-wives, the department chairman-
ship, and a credibility gap."

"It wasn't all there in black-and-white?"

"It took forever to sort out McFerrin's mess," Gregory says. "I
couldn't make heads or tails of his instructions. Petrovsky saved my
skin a hundred times over during the course of this fiasco. He can-

celled a whole troop of Girl Scouts so that the senior seminar in gal-
axies could get in for the Saturn images this evening. He set up a
panel discussion on Saturn's moons for tomorrow morning, to pla-
cate the Girl Scouts. It's grim to owe your sacred skin to a graduate
student. Especially if it's Petrovsky."

He picks up a spoon from the table and stirs his coffee. "Mc-
Ferrin's probably having a vodka with Carl Sagan in the Caltech
faculty club right now," he says.

"Carl Sagan drinks vodka?"

"Right at this very moment," Gregory says. "I can see McFerrin, casually leaning against the bar, while Sagan sips his vodka—"

"Gregory, Carl Sagan drinks vodka?"

"I think McFerrin's still bitter because he narrowly missed
discovering that moon. 'I wish you *had* found the moon,' I told
him. 'Gregory,' he said, 'it was inevitable that you find the moon.
Your line of research was simply more elegant, your pursuit of
Saturn more ardent. Among astronomers your prediction of the existence of that moon by a slight perturbation in the orbit of the
eleventh moon is considered something of a stroke of genius. When
we hired you we spoke of you as our *Wunderkind*, the bright
hope of our future. It is unreasonable for you, now that you have
worked in the department for two years, to continue your pre-
tense of naiveté.' "

"McFerrin talked to you like that?"

"Ha," Gregory says. "That's classic McFerrin. Bitter." He
drops the spoon; it narrowly misses his saucer. "I can see McFerrin
now," he says. "Asking Sagan casually if he wants his olive."

Yesterday, when Gregory called me, I was startled to hear his voice.
The last time we had seen each other was only two days after the
divorce, in a soundproof rehearsal room in the music hall. He must
have absent-mindedly walked into the wrong room, because he
looked surprised to see me there, pantomimed a sort of Charlie
Chaplin walk across the floor, banged his head against the far wall

silently, and left, closing the door gently. Perhaps he would have tried to talk to me, I thought later, if I had taken my mouth from the reed of the oboe. Perhaps he would have told me then that Natalie was moving in with him that week, and that he was beginning to have doubts.

When he said on the telephone that he wanted me to come with him for the *Voyager I* broadcasts in the planetarium, I must have sounded doubtful. These images of Saturn would be a once-in-a-lifetime thing, he explained; we could make an evening of it. Natalie was in northern Minnesota, performing Bach at a school for deaf children.

"You're crazy," I said. "Bach for deaf children?"

"It's one of Natalie's theories," he said. "I can't interpret the dynamics of it—not the way she can. You should hear her. She thinks that handicapped children can establish a kind of intimacy with the music if the environment is sufficiently supportive."

"She's taking money to do this?"

"It all depends on the highly human, nurturant quality of the environment. That's the crucial thing, for the pianist to establish an almost telepathic rapport."

"Gregory," I said. "Deaf is deaf."

He paused. "We've never really been very good on the telephone, have we?"

"No," I said. "We never have."

"Listen, I think you should come. I mean that I want you to come, Jennifer. I think that it would be good for you to get out. You've become a sort of recluse."

"Yes. The phantom oboist."

"We haven't seen each other for six months."

"More like twelve," I said. "And that's sort of the point of a divorce."

"Twelve?" he said. "You mean it's been a year?"

"I've never liked the way you lose track of things, Gregory," I said.

"What things?"

"Time," I said. "Sometimes a wife. Details."

I was pleased to find that I had replaced the receiver quite gently in its cradle. I looked around me; the telephone was by my left knee, silent. I was sitting cross-legged on the floor. When the telephone rang again, I jumped, knocking my knee against it.

"Jennifer?" he said. "Don't hang up. I know you think I didn't take your music seriously."

I bit my lower lip, saying nothing.

"There was a long while when I wasn't very happy—it wasn't your fault. It wasn't that I was unhappy exactly, except that nothing ever seemed to crystallize."

"It's hard," I said. "When you can't keep discovering moons."

"It had nothing to do with the moon."

"Everything after that was sort of anticlimactic for you."

"No," he said desperately. "It was me. I had lost a sense of direction."

"I wouldn't count Natalie as a sense of direction," I said. "She barely has one."

"There were other things going wrong—"

The receiver fit neatly into the cradle. I was pleased with this fact. I lifted the receiver again. I was pleased with the dial tone. I nudged the telephone with my knee, to see if there would be any response. There was none. The telephone is on the floor, as is the bed. There are no chairs. The walls of the trailer are panelled in some kind of thin dark wood that splinters whenever you try to drive a nail into it. My photographs are lined up along the baseboard: the mountains in Switzerland, myself standing bravely on the steps of Juilliard, the profile of an elderly cellist with whom I was once briefly in love. The trailer is in the mountains. It belongs to a graduate student who got a grant to study an infection of the respiratory systems of llamas. I met him at a fund-raising supper one evening, and went home with him that night. He said the infection was endangering the economies of several remote Peruvian villages. These subsistence-level economies, he said, relied entirely on the llama. When I said that I envied them, he only looked at me, puzzled. He was leaving the next week. I agreed—on the spur of the moment, and under the influence of a certain amount of gin—to take the trailer for a couple of weeks, until I could find someone to house-sit for him. He went through the trailer with me, turning faucets on and off, lighting the stove. It seemed the first definite decision I had made after the divorce, and I felt vaguely proud. My knees no longer ache with the hours of sitting cross-legged, the oboe balanced correctly, my music propped against the photograph of the Alps. The student sends snapshots of the llamas; they seem intelligent and world-weary. I wrote him that I am thinking of getting a dog. I imagine a small dog with a calm, quizzical expression, its head resting lightly on my knee while I practice. The graduate student answered my letter quickly. It might be better, he wrote, to consider something practical—a German shepherd or Doberman pinscher. After all, you are a woman living alone in the mountains.

When the phone rang again, I sat as still as possible, as if that would make a difference. He can't be sure I am still here, I thought. The phone rang nineteen times, and stopped. When it started to ring again, I picked it up.

"Jennifer?" he said gently.

"You've always had more endurance, haven't you?"

"It's not a contest," he said. "I still think of you. All the time."

"Gregory," I whispered. "Go away. Really. Go somewhere far away."

I pushed the telephone with my foot, until it rested against the wall, wedged between Switzerland and the rumpled bed. I examined it to determine how the cord was connected to the telephone, but I couldn't figure it out. I heaped old copies of *National Geographic* on it, staring at the covers: oval houses made of bamboo, women wearing necklaces of amber. I studied the face of a Sienese woman, the wide competent mouth, the tilt of the cheekbones; she probably had had five husbands, and all of them content. I rubbed my face furiously with the back of my hand; it came away wet, and smudged with mascara.

When I called Gregory back this morning to tell him that I

would come after all, he was surprised. "What made you change your mind?" he said.

"I don't know," I said.

The Volvo skidded on the icy road down from the mountains. I nearly rear-ended a huge truck marked "Colorado Boneless Beef." "God, you look wonderful," Gregory said when I stood in the doorway. I backed away from him, confused. For a moment I thought he was going to kiss me, but he only nodded for me to come inside.

It is now almost dark in the kitchen. Gregory leans forward, his long legs wrapped around the rungs of his architect's stool, blowing on his coffee. He is squinting slightly. I can see the fine lines in the corners of his eyes. Ten years ago, when we were first married, Gregory had nightmares in which his sight suddenly blurred or darkened; he dreamed of cataracts, of long and delicate operations that were not successful. I would wake to find him sitting in his pajamas, turning the pages of a book of paintings by Vermeer, running his fingers across the faces of the women, the panes in the windows. In the morning, he would dress, packing frayed sweaters and a stocking cap into an old briefcase. He drove to the observatory directly from the university, after his last class. The telescope with which he was working then was nearly as long as a Greyhound bus, tilted at an inquisitive angle toward the sky. The maintenance of the telescope's internal workings required a degree of cold that could numb your fingers. You could see the janitor's breath as he waxed the tile floors of the observatory at night. While Gregory did his observations—each one lasting two or three hours—he would listen to Rachmaninoff. He thought Rachmaninoff was lucky. The janitor would change the records, handling each disk with great tenderness because his hands were cold. Gregory barely moved. He was held in a kind of cradle at the end of the telescope, as stiff with clothing as a child on a sled.

The night he observed the hidden moon—it was gone in the

blink of an eye, he said, but he had seen it, it was fitful and clear as a firefly—the janitor had poured champagne over Gregory's head until his hair was in his eyes. I licked the champagne from the edges of his mustache when he kissed me. The janitor and I danced a rough approximation of a waltz while Gregory conducted Rachmaninoff. "What will you name the moon?" I asked him over the janitor's thin shoulder. The janitor held me stiffly, nearly a foot away from his chest. We turned and spun. "I don't know," Gregory said. "Moons are named by committees now, I think. This committee is now in session. Anyone have any ideas?"

It is still a secret; only the three of us are supposed to know that the moon was named for the night janitor.

"Jennifer," Gregory says. "Shall we go?"

When he opens the front door, Natalie's cat slips between his legs into the darkness. "Damn," Gregory says. "She's not supposed to go out when it's this cold." He stands on the front stairs, looking perplexed. Snow stings my eyelids, the corners of my mouth.

"Will she come back if we wait?"

"I doubt it. This is a truly neurotic cat. She will only come back into the house through the attic window. To get into the attic window she climbs the tree. When it's as windy as this she can't climb the tree, and I'll be damned if I'm going to miss the first images of Saturn because I'm hunting for that cat." He looks at his wrist, where his watch is hidden under several layers of clothing.

"The attic window's open?"

"Not really," he says. "It's broken." When we first moved into the house I had painted all the floors and rafters in the attic white, and put old Persian rugs on the walls. I practiced the oboe there. "I was going to fix it, darling, but there was this Saturn thing," he says. He puts one gloved hand lightly on my shoulder. "I think we should go," he says.

"Will she be all right?"

"Sure," he says. "That cat's as ingenious as she is perverse."

He shoves the front door with his shoulder—it has never quite closed right, and the lock sometimes sticks.

The quadrangle in the center of the campus is dark. On the sidewalks, students appear in shafts of light, their faces partially shrouded by the haze of their breath in the cold air, and disappear again into the darkness. Two joggers wearing phosphorescent earmuffs run by, singing "We're off to see the Wizard" in unison. Gregory takes me through a maze of side streets. "This is my shortcut," he explains. "Somewhere, in one of these alleys, a thief is walking in a beautiful fur coat." The dome of the planetarium is filmed with falling snow. Outside the glass entranceway, there is a huge silver disk resting at an angle in the snow; it is nearly as tall as a man, sleek and concave. Gregory goes to it, running his gloved hand meditatively across the surface. "They don't guard it or anything," he says. "Isn't that amazing? This is receiving transmissions from the planet Saturn."

"By way of Pasadena."

"Yes." He grins suddenly. "You know what, Jennifer? I want one of these for Christmas." He draws the glove from his hand and strokes the gleaming metal with bare fingers. "Feel," he says, touching me on the cheek.

"Stick your tongue to it. I dare you."

"It's that mysterious cold."

"What cold?"

"The cold of great distances," he says.

Inside the glass doors, steering me through the crowd of people, he puts his arm across my shoulders. "Natalie would hate this," he says. "She can't stand crowds, unless they've come to listen to her."

The first time I ever saw Natalie was at a winter costume party where a man in a white-rabbit suit was drunkenly banging out "Papa Haydn" on an ancient piano. Natalie had come as Amelia Earhart. She stood in a corner of the room, fingering the knot of her silk scarf anxiously, while near her two tenors discussed Listerine. When I turned—Gregory was beginning an impassioned description of the craters of Ganymede—Natalie was rushing from the room. The white rabbit was staring after her. "All I was doing was playing 'Papa Haydn!' " he shouted. "Is that a crime, Natalie? Is that a *crime?*" As she pushed toward the doorway Natalie paused, caught for a moment between Gregory and the doorjamb. "I just can't deal with his insensitivity anymore," she said. Gregory stared at her. Her skin was flushed below the rims of the aviator goggles. "God, you're beautiful," she said. "Whose are you?" The rabbit was making his unsteady way toward her through the crowd. When he reached the doorway, Natalie was gone. A cold wind blew into the room. Someone shouted at the rabbit to close the door, but he stood there, looking apprehensive, until Gregory asked him, "Who was that?" "That was my wife," the rabbit said. He went through the doorway and stood looking up and down the street in the falling snow. Natalie was nowhere in sight. The rabbit trudged slowly across the lawn and climbed into a battered white Volkswagen. The engine knocked faintly and died. After a few minutes it started up again; the white rabbit got out and cleaned the snow from the windshield with his paw. There was a bumper sticker on the dented bumper: "Musicians Make Better Lovers."

"They ought to get Natalie one of those little cyanide capsules," said one of the tenors. "Then every time it got too rough for her with Albert, she could just hold the little capsule under her nose. It would really save on gas."

"Well, it solves one mystery," the second tenor said. "At least now we know what the White Rabbit was chasing."

After that, Natalie courted Gregory. She discovered which mailbox in the departmental office was his and filled it with animal crackers. She telephoned at odd hours. She left a series of funny photographs of herself—Natalie dancing, Natalie dressed as a mime—under the asteroid fragment on his desk. She became fluent about the revolutions of the planets, the spectrum of visible light, the origins of quasars. For a long while, Gregory would get stoned in his office among the models of the planets, then cross the campus to the music hall, where I was practicing late. He would sometimes look wistfully down to the far end of the hall, where Natalie was practicing Bartók in a large, empty room with Kandinsky posters on the walls. Albert wrote me a note and left it one night on my music stand: "What's blond and blue-eyed and waits patiently with its head in the sand?" I turned the note over twice before I realized that he had written no answer. Natalie moved out of Albert's apartment in one night, stripping the walls of the Indonesian baskets that she collected. Albert went into Jungian analysis; Natalie went on tour; Gregory caught a bad cold. For the first time, he failed two graduate students in his astrophysics class. "They were too smug," he said. "Astronomers have to be capable of being surprised." Gregory could not sleep; he stayed awake all night in his study, slowly turning the pages of his Vermeer book. When he finally told me that he wanted a divorce, I sat awake nearly all night on the lawn, staring at the darkened house as if I had never seen it before, the oboe cradled in the lap of my nightgown. When I climbed the stairs to the bedroom, my feet were very cold. I laid the oboe carefully on the floor. "What's the matter?" Gregory said. He was surprised that I had come back to the bed. "You're shaking like a leaf, Jennifer."

"How do you know I won't murder you?" I whispered. "How do you know I won't find the two of you together and set fire to the house?"

He said nothing. I could tell he was wide awake.

"How do you know I won't go out into the woods and lose all my clothes and become a feral child?"

He turned to face me. "You can't," he said quietly. "You're too old to become a feral child, and even if there were wolves, they wouldn't adopt you." He closed his eyes tightly while I was still staring at him in the dark. I closed my eyes tightly, too. When I was a child I was suspicious; I thought that people could still sense what was going on through their eyelids. I never felt safe around people with their eyes closed. Now, in case Gregory could see me, I smiled quietly, reassuringly, to show him that I would never burn the house down.

I encountered Natalie only once after the divorce. It was in the downtown supermarket, and she was peering into a glass case at a row of organic chickens.

"Natalie?" I said.

"God," Natalie said. "You startled me."

"I didn't mean to." I looked through the glass case at the chickens. "It's getting expensive, isn't it?"

"What is?" she said. "Do you mean the chicken, or what?" She backed away, shaking her head. "I can't handle this," she said. She backed down the aisle and disappeared, leaving her shopping cart. I studied it for a moment. It contained five quarts of Perrier, a bunch of parsley, and a roll of Scotch Magic Transparent tape. Poor Gregory, I thought.

One evening not long after that, Albert stood in the doorway of the music room, his shoulder against the doorjamb. "Guess what loving couple is suddenly having trouble?" he asked.

"I don't want to hear about it, Albert," I said. I rested the reed of the oboe between my tongue and my teeth.

"It's all right for you," he said. "You can hide in your oboe. I must say you look terrific. Do you want me to take you to lunch, so that you can have one decent meal this week?"

"No, thanks," I said. The truth was that every time I looked at Albert I saw him desperately cleaning the windshield of the Volkswagen with his paw. I wanted to be as far removed from that desperation as possible.

"Really, I'd be glad to," Albert said. "They're having some serious problems. Natalie called me in the middle of the night last night—"

"Albert," I said. I blew an experimental A.

"O.K.," he said. "I'm going." He stood and shrugged slightly.

"Your A's a little off," he said. "Well, you can never say you weren't warned."

"Look at all the people," Gregory whispers. "I called this morning and asked Petrovsky how we were doing. 'Great, sir,' he said. 'You're slated for moderator of that panel tomorrow morning. Some photographers from the paper may show up. Sir, do you have a tuxedo? I thought it might be amusing if you wore a tuxedo.' Petrovsky likes to accentuate my eccentricity, you see."

"Poor Petrovsky. Transmuted from child genius into head usher."

"He loves it. You know what Natalie told me? 'You should never put a Virgo in charge of anything like this.' "

"Petrovsky is a Virgo?"

"I don't know. Natalie knows. I don't think even Petrovsky knows."

Petrovsky makes his way toward us through the crowd. He is thin, wearing a Star Wars T-shirt and tattered Adidas. His hair is the color of Raggedy Andy's. "There you are, Dr. K.," he says. He nods at me. I have never counted for much in Petrovsky's vision of things. "I've been hoping nothing happened to hold you up," he says.

"A small accident," Gregory says.

"Nothing serious, I hope?"

"A cat escaping into the snow."

"Ah." Petrovsky is clearly at a loss.

Gregory strokes my cheek with his glove. "Why don't you find us some seats, Petrovsky?"

Petrovsky leads us into the darkened interior of the planetarium; in the dimly lit doorways, various ushers stare upward at the curve of the dome. Petrovsky edges down the aisle, stooping to shine his flashlight at the numbered plaques on the seats. "Here we are, sir," Petrovsky says. Gregory guides me into my seat, then takes his own. Petrovsky nods again, this time at the two of us. He covers the beam of his flashlight politely with his hand.

"Petrovsky," Gregory says. "Thank you. May I ask you a personal question?"

"Certainly."

"Petrovsky, do you consider Carl Sagan more photogenic than I am?"

Petrovsky blinks. His expression is one of dazzled reverence. The light of the flashlight shines through his fingers, illuminating the slender bones. For the last two years, he has been covertly making preliminary notes for a biography of Gregory.

"No way, sir," Petrovsky says.

The curve of the planet is luminous and huge. Three-quarters of the way down it is sliced by the shadows of the rings, pitch-black and straight as a highway across the cloud field. The picture is framed by the illumined grid within which the computer displays each momentary image of the planet. Saturn seems radiant, like a football field under the lights before the first man has run across it.

"They're getting enormous amounts of non-visual data, so between the pictures they're just going to talk," Gregory says. "Look, there's old Seligmann. That's really odd. I thought that he was dead." The narrator, Seligmann, is a frail man in a crumpled gray suit. His straight black tie is patterned with satellites, and it seems to anchor him in place. He stares calmly at an immense notebook on the table before him. The notebook is filled with charts and columns of precise handwriting. "He probably misses his chalk and blackboard," Gregory says. "He used to draw the most beautiful diagrams of the constellations, all in colored chalk. They were so lovely that the cleaning women would leave them overnight."

The narrator coughs. "You have to understand that what you are seeing here is a sphere of cloud in constant flight," he says. "The cloud patterning is enormously complex—longitudinal islands of cloud, so to speak, around which there are swirls and eddies of absolute chaos. Some features come and go with clockwork regularity, other configurations have endured for what would be, in earthly terms, incredible periods of time. There are a number of things here which we had not entirely expected—"

"You know, I think Natalie is probably leaving me," Gregory says.

"The wind speed alone renders this planet—"

"For a harpsichordist. Named Yale. He smokes those little chocolate-colored cigarettes all the time—"

"In the realm of the fabulous."

"I think I know him, Gregory."

"He always thought he was homosexual. Until he met Natalie."

"Or what was previously *thought* to have been the fabulous."

"He has a way of laying his hands on the keys. I remember that."

"That's him. He says she's changed his life—"

"I'm sorry?"

A crescent-shaped slice of the planet appears on the screen. Its light reflects from the upturned faces of the people in the planetarium.

On the way home, in the silent quadrangle, Gregory suddenly halts.

"There's enough light to see by, isn't there?" he asks.

"Barely."

"The snow is deep enough, isn't it?"

"Deep enough for what?"

"You wait here," he says. He lopes awkwardly away from me, slowing where he hits the drifts, running in a huge circle perhaps fifty yards in diameter. Then, his breath rising in a white cloud, he runs across the diameter of the circle. He turns and crosses his first line with another, at right angles; his circle is now neatly quartered. I stand still, thinking of the cold in my hands, the blue sparks by which the Volvo will either start or fail to start, the snow collecting on the cement-block stairs in front of the trailer. Gregory trots swiftly in a second circle, inside the first one. His breath is coming raggedly now.

"Fox-and-goose!" he shouts. "Or don't you remember?"

He stamps the last few feet of his circle.

"Gregory!" I shout. "I'm exhausted."

"I'm tired from running the circles," he shouts. "That will give you the advantage."

I walk slowly to the perimeter of the outer circle. I will be the goose, he the fox. The tamped snow squeaks beneath my boots. He faces me from the very center of the circle, where the lines intersect. He claps his hands together to warm them; even in the darkness I can tell that he never takes his eyes from my face.

He has to run on the lines. Those are the rules.

THE

EVOLUTION

OF BIRDS OF

PARADISE

The *Ptiloris victoriae* has been stealing kitchen matches. The vanilla-white wood of perhaps a hundred matchsticks is visible within the dark weave of her nest, a knobbed oval wedged between two tilted volumes of the 1954 edition of the *Universal Standard Encyclopedia.* Simon thinks she has chosen handsomely: the encyclopedia spines, although lean and somewhat frayed, are still upright, the dusty covers stamped with magic lanterns. One page—in Volume 15, *Idah-Jewe*—is marked with a flattened orchid whose mummified pistil furls upward like a lizard's tongue, scholarly and dry. Simon tries to remember what continent he retrieved this flower from; he closes his eyes and sees only an island of reeds, the kinked tip of a crocodile's tail vanishing among them.

The desk itself is teak, and the nest spills forward across it in a prow of splayed twigs, partially burying a chambered nautilus and an ancient Bic pen with a splintered tip. Simon studies the massed papers. Lately he has tried to shuffle them into a parallel-edged heap, but they falter into disorder, acquire the linked sienna rings of coffee-cup stains, crinkle at the edges. Above him, there is the thudding of bare feet. Ashley, his daughter-in-law, always runs down the stairs, although he has lectured frostily on the danger —the narrow treads, the steep, old-fashioned angle of descent. Once, she did fall, and hit her forehead against the bannister, her hair fanning across the threadbare carpet. Somehow Simon felt it was his fault: without his scrutiny, in a realm beyond his anxious old man's predictions, she was blithe, infallible. She had stayed obediently still, eyes closed, while he washed the blood away with a wetted handkerchief.

"Your handkerchief, Simon," she protested, when she opened her eyes. "You're ruining it."

"It doesn't matter," he said.

"It does matter," she said. "It's an antique."

Startled, he looked down to see that the yellowing linen still bore the tracery of his name, which Anna had long ago cross-stitched in neat X's of shining thread. Anna had packed and left him thirty-four years ago, while he was in the field. He had returned to find a house magically bare of all signs of life. In her precise fashion, she had even removed their wedding picture from the wall, and plastered over the hole. He had picked at the patch of new plaster with his thumbnail and, when it refused to flake away, driven the blade of a kitchen knife into it. He had needed to reassure himself that the hole existed, that it had held the nail supporting a photograph— Anna, smiling sideways at him, her dark eyes expectant. His own face, even then, was narrow, the corners of the mouth bracketed by skeptical lines. The photographer had airbrushed the nick in his chin—his shaving, that distant morning, had been impatient—but he could do nothing to render the ill-fitting tuxedo more elegant, or smooth the badly cut hair from Simon's forehead. Anna's hand, in the photograph, rested trustingly in the crook of his elbow. It was true: she had expected something of him, and he had failed her.

"I've looked in the Salvation Army," Ashley said. "You just

can't find these anymore." She was examining the crescents of the embroidered capitals.

"Keep it, if you like," he said. She looked at him guiltily; she had already thrust one corner into the pocket of her Levi's.

It is only through a foible of the National Science Foundation that Ashley lives in his house at all: the money came through for his son's research, and not for hers. Their subsequent strategy—nearly a year spent apart, with Michael exchanging the classrooms of the University of Colorado for an Army surplus tent pitched not far from Machu Picchu, while Ashley continued to teach—seems to Simon fraught with incalculable risk. For Michael, the haunting symmetries of ancient cities—tombs as deep as alleys, amulets on the slim dry wrists of skeletons—are an overwhelming passion, but Simon has observed evidence of uncertainty in Ashley. She bites her fingernails; her lecture notes for "An Introduction to Early Man in North America" are scribbled at the last moment, on the backs of grocery lists or torn telephone bills; she has put two small dents in the fenders of Michael's Fiat. "Why don't you go live with my father?" Michael had said. "We could use the money you'd save, and he has this huge old house where he rattles around all alone, and it makes him a little crazy. He could keep an eye on you, and you'd be terrific for him. You could keep him in touch with reality." "What makes you think I have any patent on reality?" Ashley said, but nonetheless she had come, settling her books into the shelves in Michael's old upstairs bedroom, wiping the dust from the crooked brass headboard of the bed.

Now Simon lifts a Peruvian flute from among the manuscripts— a wand of dark wood, rubbed and scratched, ringed with flaking gold leaf. He blows experimentally. A feather of dust lifts from the other end, startling the *Ptiloris victoriae*, Queen Victoria Riflebird, which has at that moment alighted on the crown of his bald head. Her feet are skittish and cool; he feels the claws as a scattering of hesitant pricks against his scalp. Awkwardly, he stoppers the holes of the flute. His knuckles seem far too large for such precise maneuvering. When he was twenty-two he once fished a splinter from a cannibal's eye: the flat black disk of the pupil had held the reflection of Simon's hand, perfectly miniaturized, and the inside of the lid was the vulnerable, breathing coral of a trout's gill. In gratitude the cannibal had kissed Simon's knuckles. When he was thirty-four Simon could hold a curved, blue-gray fragment of eggshell, flecked with dirty-cinnamon spots, into a shaft of light filtering through the rain-forest canopy and name the female bird of paradise that had, until recently, sheltered it. At forty Simon could hear bones forming in the egg of a wren. At eighty-two, when the Queen Victoria's weight is gone from his head, he feels as if a crown has been removed. Ashley never sees the birds, but this has ceased to bother Simon, as long as she does not blunder into a courtship display, or drop one of her muddy running shoes into the gnarled fretwork of twigs and reeds belonging to a nesting female.

The Queen Victoria jumps to his desk, carrying a twig, this one long and forked and bearing one coppery leaf. It must be from the aspen tree to the left of the back door. The aspen lost all of its leaves early this winter, and is certainly dying. Three times, Simon has considered cutting the tree down, and each time decided against it, in part because the straight lower branch still holds the two uneven lengths of rope, fraying and always damp, that once held the yellow board on which Michael had spent whole afternoons swinging, his legs lifting and falling loosely. Whenever Simon rests the blade of the ax against the silver bark he seems to hear the double creak of the vanished swing—two notes, one for ascent, one for the downward arc.

The placement of the twig puzzles the Queen Victoria. Simon sees that the nest is nearly finished; the innermost hollow precisely accords with the span of her breast. She will be guarded by this structure the way, in fairy tales, princesses are guarded by walls of thorns. If this were New Guinea she would have searched out a snakeskin to decorate it. She tucks the twig into a gap between strands of gray lichen and, dissatisfied, thrusts it in farther. Two eggs, Simon thinks, of a color paler than the interior of a conch shell, and far more frail. He knocks on wood. The Queen Victoria

disappears into the steeple-shaped shadow between the two ency-
clopedias.

"I have a bone to pick with you, Simon," Ashley says from the
doorway of his study. She has on a pair of Levi's that Michael long
ago abandoned, held at the waist by a beaded belt that says "New
Mexico." The belt is buckled at the very last notch. She is wearing
a black sweatshirt with the sleeves pushed up above her elbows, and
a John Deere cap pulled down to shadow her eyes. The leaping deer
on the front of the cap mimics the arch of one eyebrow. Even her
name, he sometimes thinks, is simply one more aspect of the an-
drogyny in which young women camouflage themselves nowadays.
He has never actually questioned her—why did her parents inflict
such a name upon the innocent, feathery blond curve of her infant
skull?—preserving, for once, the crafty patriarchal silence he
equates with dignity in a father-in-law.

"Oh?" he says. "What bone would that be?"

"You amaze me, you know," she says. "Two wars, treks into the
interior of New Guinea when it was still riddled with headhunters, a
couple of tropical diseases, and you still think that knocking on
wood will ward off dangers."

"Three wars," he says. "I was an adviser in the Korean war."

"An adviser?"

"Someone had the bright idea of reintroducing carrier pigeons."

"Oh."

"Not a handsome bird, exactly." After his years spent in the
pursuit of birds of paradise, the pigeons had seemed muddling, qui-
escent, ash-colored. "But they have made a sort of virtue of self-
possession. They can find their way through clouds of smoke, and
they're not easily rattled."

"I didn't know you'd been involved in something like that."

"It was years ago," he says. "So you think that an old man ought
to relinquish superstition? Ought to be dispassionate about his
fate?"

"I can't imagine you dispassionate."

"You can't? A growing introspection, a calm renunciation of my failing powers?" He holds his hands, palm upward, for her inspection, and is briefly amused to find the fingers trembling. He has always gotten carried away in proving his own points. "Nothing up my sleeve, Madam."

Beneath the bill of the skewed man's cap her eyes seem to go a shade darker. He admires her eyebrows: feather-shaped, the outer tips seeming faintly smudged. "I have yet to see you renounce anything," she says. "You, introspective? It's a contradiction in terms. You've had a finger in every pie for decades—at least every pie that had anything to do with birds."

"Four-and-twenty blackbirds," Simon says.

"Don't go whimsical on me, O.K.?" she says. "Just last week you nearly sent poor Dr. Cooper into cardiac arrest over the taxonomy of birds of paradise. It's not enough that the two of you have been quarreling since 1924. You have to go and torment him while he's flat on his back in an oxygen tent."

"I went to see him," he says cautiously. "You know that I intended it as a gesture of professional courtesy. I wouldn't have attempted it five years ago, because there were other people around then who were simply better at that sort of thing than I, people who can sit in those gummy metal hospital chairs and contentedly play gin rummy, or discourse on moods in falling snow—"

"You wouldn't touch a deck of cards to save your life," she says. "And if you ever did play gin rummy, it would be so that you could beat him. You must have provoked him, Simon."

"I only observed that the ancestral stock of the birds of paradise was undoubtedly starlinglike," he says. "What happened after that wasn't my fault."

Cooper had sat up against his crisp pillows, enraged. "How can you stand there and spout that crap to me as if it's gospel?" he had shouted. "Next you'll be questioning the existence of the arboreal monogamous ancestors!"

"I am leaning toward polygyny," Simon had confessed. "It will mean redrawing the family tree, at first, but I do find myself increasingly disenchanted with the idea of those monogamous pairs of ancestors blown down the East Indian archipelago by various punctual hurricanes."

"They had to get to New Guinea somehow," Cooper roared. "It's an island, for the love of God!"

"Starlings are such interesting birds, though, aren't they? Brainy and, in an evolutionary sense, so willing to try anything once."

"You're too late. You can't rewrite the whole of *The Evolution of Birds of Paradise*. You're too old."

Simon obligingly spread his knuckly hands. The veins on the backs were the color of slate, and there were various spots and flecks. He is growing dappled. "I am old," he said. Cooper shook his head irritably, as if that were an obvious lie. "It doesn't take a lot to keep me awake," Simon went on. "I eat Cheerios while I watch the ten-o'clock news, and I get to watch the sun come up. I am of course prepared to take on a substantial amount of observation in the field."

"In the field?" Cooper said.

"In the field."

"But the field is New Guinea," Cooper said.

Simon cleared his throat softly.

"That's utterly impossible," Cooper said. "A man of your age, the frailty of your hands. Isn't there something wrong with your heart as well?"

"No," Simon said. "Not a damn thing wrong with my heart." But Cooper had already subsided into a long, unwavering, absent-minded stare. Simon remembered the cannibal's eye, clearing suddenly, enormous and patient. Cooper, although looking directly at him, had forgotten he was there.

"It was your fault, and you know it," Ashley says.

"Maybe," he amends, because she is still studying him, "I was also, in part, moved by curiosity. I wanted to see how he was doing it."

"Doing what?"

"Dying," he says. If he thinks this will daunt her, he is clearly mistaken.

"So why did you take him milkweed pods? When I telephoned to find out why you were late getting home, the nurse said you were carrying a whole armful of weeds that you dropped on the bedside table. You didn't even wait for her to bring a vase."

"I know it seems strange," he says. "But I've always found them beautiful, like small gray canoes filled with bleached silk." Thoughtfully, he moves a chipped glass paperweight across the dusty teak. Within the encyclopedia-framed gap, a black eye gleams. "Cooper spent more than thirty years in the field. In one of our rare amicable moments we were comparing horror stories, and he topped me, told me how he had once lived for a week on water stored in an enormous hollowed-out ostrich egg that had been given to him by a friendly aborigine. He said the water at first was bitter, then it started to have a medicinal taste, and the last few swallows went down like wine. Now, what would a man like that want with narcissi?"

"I don't know," she says.

"I can tell you," he says. "Nothing. Nothing at all."

An hour later, Simon is standing on a kitchen chair changing a light bulb as Ashley answers the telephone in the hallway. Her demurral seems courteous and contrived, perhaps for his benefit, and when she finally acquiesces, the person at the other end of the line cannot have been astonished. "Somebody must have broken a leg," she calls to Simon. "Because I've just gotten invited to the Petersons' for the evening."

"It wouldn't require a broken leg, surely?"

"They're snobs," she says. "They like to collect defectors from Soviet-bloc countries, escapees from the Moonies, ex-convicts. Not WASP associate professors of anthropology. I'll have to go and change." She runs—still barefoot, skipping every two steps—up the flight of wooden stairs to her room. When she comes back down, he sees that she has changed into a black dress with a shallow neckline. One strap is twisted clumsily, like that of a child's bathing suit. Yearning rises from the pit of Simon's stomach; the back of his throat tastes coarsely of rust. She is wearing a string of amber, one of his many tentative gifts of rapprochement to Anna, which Anna wore once and then abandoned, because, she told him, it made her neck look "blunt." He had thought it made her look queenly. Ashley appropriated it, another of the childlike confiscations with which she unsettles his house. She sits, careless of the dress, in a straight-backed oak chair at the kitchen table. Abruptly the male *Paradisaea minor,* Lesser Bird of Paradise, lights on her bare shoulder. Simon halts for a moment to look down. The Lesser Bird of Paradise cocks its head to gaze back at him. The iris of its eye is a clear lime yellow. "The chair is wobbling, Simon."

"It's all right."

"It's too old to stand on like that—"

"I'm sure it's quite reliable."

"Would you like me to hold it for you?"

"No, please don't get up."

"I can't live here forever without lifting a finger."

"You can hardly believe you've lived here forever," he says. Her hyperbole sometimes stings his sense of exactitude. Simon believes that politeness is more or less a variation of accuracy.

"No," she says. "I mean that you shouldn't have to do all the work for both of us."

"I do precious little more than I would for myself, alone," he says. He tinkers with the light bulb. He is reluctant to twist it the rest of the way in, fearing that when he does she will get up, disturbing the Lesser Bird of Paradise, which is notoriously shy. He has not had nearly enough time to observe it. He is pleased to see that the curved barbs of the long white tail feathers are utterly free of lice. Snowy, neat, and separate, they fall between Ashley's shoulder blades, brushing the back of her chair. Before she came, he had sighted only blackbirds, sparrows, and an occasional nightjar or marsh hen—nothing that excited his professional interest. After Michael had gone, and she had been in the house only two weeks, Simon found ferns unfurling like sea horses from the cracks between the floorboards, and brilliant feathers strayed into his pockets. He had retrieved his old pair of binoculars from the back of a closet shelf, dusted off their lenses, and taken to wearing them around his chest, where their cool remembered weight balanced like a second, steadier heart.

The Lesser Bird of Paradise's tail feathers flick in agitation. It shifts to keep its balance while Ashley lights a cigarette. Its wings slant forward, the feathers extending in a dovetailed curve, like the paper of a fan stiffening between oblique ribs. It holds this pose, stiff with ardor or apprehension, within a haze of slowly rising cigarette smoke. "Simon, aren't you done yet?"

"Done." He dusts his palms against his trousers. "Stay like that, would you?"

"Why should I?"

"I was thinking what Michael would give to see you like this."

"Oh? What would Michael give?"

"His right arm," Simon says. "Willingly."

"I'm not as sure as you are," she says. "He hasn't written for nearly two months. The last letter he wrote was from Cuzco. He was sitting at a cafe table, reading *A Farewell to Arms* and drinking espresso. He said *A Farewell to Arms* wasn't as good as he remembered."

Simon gives the bulb in its socket a final, extraneous twist, proving—he hopes—his extreme care. He intends it as a sort of reproof. She inhales cigarette smoke; the lesson is lost on her. He climbs down from the chair, and drops the burned bulb into the paper bag below the sink.

"I suppose you think it's silly of me to want to go out in all this snow," she says.

"Not necessarily," he says. "A great deal of valuable information was exchanged at faculty parties even in my era."

It is one of their problems: they often begin to apologize at the same moment, and abandon the attempt out of mutual embarrassment. She twists the cigarette out in a small, violent spiral in the bottom of the ashtray and sees him watching. "Maybe I ought to give up smoking for one of my New Year's resolutions," she says.

"Excellent idea."

"There's a big difference, you know, Simon. You were famous in your era. Of course people courted you and told you things. You and McPherson virtually discovered the birds of paradise—"

"That's inaccurate, as you very well know."

"It must have been extraordinary to observe their courtship in the rain forest when you knew no one had ever seen anything like that before. Michael thinks you've never quite gotten over it."

"Michael believes in getting over things."

"And you don't?"

"Sometimes not. There are certain things I wouldn't want to get over."

For a moment he observes her: the thin shoulder, the fine shading of the eyelids, the glint of vein in her wrist. The Lesser Bird of Paradise seems frozen on her shoulder. Only its golden eye blinks. Ashley lights another cigarette, after tapping it against the kitchen table. She does not seem startled to have caught him staring: she simply stares back. Then she rises to turn on the light, and the Lesser Bird of Paradise—startled, its wings doubling back toward the body, its nape suddenly dimming into shadow—takes flight, and swerves around a corner of the refrigerator and down the hallway. She sits back down and crosses her legs. He has never seen her in high heels before. He is almost certain that they are not the sort of thing a young woman ought to wear into the snow. He strains to remember Anna's shoes; his only memory is a vague one of something sullen, with a pinched tongue and bone buttons. He dismisses it hurriedly. He thinks of Ashley as a glorified tomboy, her beauty all unwitting. It pains him that she would suddenly display the fine curve of her instep in such a precarious black shoe. He leans against the counter and looks away from her, out the window. In the light from the kitchen the falling snow is dense and uneven. It seems to pause in its downward slant several inches above the ground, as if balked by the warmth the earth still casts weakly upward.

"The snow's not even sticking," she says.

"It's beginning to stick." He feels suddenly irritable.

"The driving should be all right for a while longer. It's really not all that far from here."

"I haven't seen the lights of a single snowplow," he says. "This is the very worst sort of weather to do any driving in. They don't consider a storm like this serious enough to get off their bums and start plowing. You'll hear them out about midnight, not before."

"Fine," she says. "A little after midnight, after everyone's kissed everyone, I can come home. It's New Year's Eve, Simon."

"I don't need to be told what night it is." He unscrews the lid of a jar of Skippy. It is creamy peanut butter instead of chunky, and Ashley likes chunky, but it is not his fault. He did the best he could.

In the 7-Eleven—the one store he found open when he went out earlier that evening—an old woman had been sweeping things into a ragged net shopping bag hanging by a string from the crook of her elbow: chocolate milk in pint-size wax cartons; a dented box of Count Chocula breakfast cereal; chocolate-covered graham crackers, Oreos, and Pepperidge Farm Mint Milanos; Hershey's chocolate bars; chocolate Santa Clauses in parchment-thin red-and-silver foil, left over from Christmas; one yellow and one brown bag of M&M's. Scanning the shelves, she chose a can of cat food and dropped it into her bag with the other things. Simon was watching. The old woman lifted her bag and rattled it provocatively at him, as a triumphant hunter might display a rabbit by its heels. "You're lucky you're not old," she said.

It confused him. "I'm as old as you," he said.

"You are?" She frowned. "I must say you hide it pretty well. I myself don't stand a chance. The cat wears me down. Morning, noon, and night, nag, nag, nag."

"I am old," he had said, for the second time that week, and, in the cramped aisle below the glimmering fluorescent lights, it had suddenly come true.

In the street outside the 7-Eleven, cars slid by, fans of brown slush rising behind each wheel. Crossing the street warily, Simon observed how small and crooked his house looked, its steep Victorian roof the only old-fashioned angle on the length of the block. The rest is the linear austerity of the condominiums, glass doors faintly glossed with heat, ski decks swept bare of snow; those right angles and massive slabs of pebbled cement offer insufficient habitat for even a sparrow. As Simon watched, a Count Raggi's Bird of Paradise flew slowly across one of the upstairs windows of his house. Simon balanced the paper bag in the crook of his elbow and withdrew a small notebook from his jacket pocket. It was already getting colder, and his fingers ached around the bitten pencil stub. *"Paradisaea raggiana,"* he wrote crookedly. "♂. Spectacular!" He crossed the last word out as unprofessional. He must learn to be harsher with his own lapses. The *Paradisaea raggiana* was yellow-crowned, black-breasted, with an astonishing tail of pale-apricot plumes; he could not refrain from doing a small dance step on the icy curb. Two small boys were watching him from the far corner. One of them bent and scooped a stone from the gutter. He was wearing a Darth Vader face mask. Simon thought suddenly of the Papuan New Guineans who had tattooed crescents of blue ink above the bridges of their wide noses and their flat, feminine cheekbones. The young tribesmen had had something of Darth Vader's faceted, unblinking menace. The stone caught Simon squarely between the shoulder blades. He put the pencil away and tucked the notebook securely into his pocket. He felt absurdly lucky to have made a sighting from outside the house—*P. raggiana!*—and at such an unlikely hour. "Crazy man, crazy man, pisses in an old tin can!" One of the voices was muted by the face mask. A lucky throw, Simon thought. He loped stiffly homeward, the brown paper bag under his arm.

He takes two saucers from the cupboard; he puts one peanut butter sandwich in the unchipped saucer, and deposits it gallantly in front of Ashley. "Look, Simon," she says, "we need to air our differences." He nods. He likes anything to do with air, or light. His only objection to New Guinea had been that the light in the rain forest seemed sifted, rare, and inaccessible. If he and Anna had aired their differences, perhaps she would not now be in a condominium (in her letters to Michael she calls it, affectionately, "the condo") in Miami Beach, on a narrow balcony far too high above the sea. He and Ashley have solved other problems. What had particularly dismayed her, in the beginning, was his habit of using up several jars of Vicks VapoRub in a week. She burned small wands of sandalwood incense to rid the living room of the damp, tropical taint that Simon secretly loved. He had agreed, with some reluctance, to use Vicks VapoRub in the bathroom, in modest amounts, and only on those afternoons when she is teaching.

There are still problems, although Simon considers them minor: Ashley gets telephone calls, mysterious and prolonged, quite late at night. Simon wakes in his narrow bed to the single *ching* of the receiver as she lifts it, catching it before the first complete ring. She must whisper, the telephone cradled to her jaw, facing the corner where he leaves his overshoes—an old man's pairing, toe to toe, as if a ghost stood anxiously inside the foyer. Who telephones her? He can't make out a word. McPherson used to stand amazed when Simon would pinpoint the location of a single Magnificent Bird of Paradise on a distant ridge. *"Ca cru cru cru,"* Simon would mimic, for McPherson's benefit. "He's a musical little bastard. *Diphyllodes magnificus,* in extremely good form, north by northeast, at an elevation of perhaps two hundred and fifty feet above the forest floor." "Damn," McPherson would say. "Can you really hear the bloody thing from this far away?" Who telephones her, and why does she talk so long? This ache within his rib cage, he reasons, must be a sort of paternal jealousy. It does not ease until, sometimes an hour later, she replaces the telephone receiver and—this time with cunning quiet—climbs the creaking stairs to her room.

"Simon," she says. "I've been under certain pressures—*professional* pressures, I won't bore you with them—lately, and they sometimes make me feel slightly claustrophobic. I know you've seen signs of it. I've been losing my temper entirely too often."

"I always take it with a grain of salt."

"A grain of salt the size of Antarctica," she says. She studies the smoke, which sifts toward the ceiling. "You've been very patient with me, and I've liked living here, but I dislike the feeling that you are watching over me. It's not something you're obligated to do, and it must be exhausting for you, and I sometimes find it distracting."

"Distracting?"

"Distracting."

It is, he thinks, a gentle word, more introspective than "annoying," less specific than "bothersome." He has seen her do worse, with less provocation. He looks at her with renewed admiration as she stands, brushing the front of the black dress. His sandwich, untouched, rests in the chipped dimestore saucer painted with thistles. She has left only her crusts. "I ought to get going," she says. "The Fiat will probably stall on me, and I don't want to be too late. Can I ask you something?"

"Ask," he says.

"I especially don't want you to stay awake all night long because of me."

"Why?" he says. "Do you think I've nothing better to do?"

In the hallway she lifts her coat in a clatter of empty hangers, ignoring his question. He has intended for years to clean out the closet; lying on the floor is an ancient umbrella of Anna's, dusty and tightly furled, which Anna somehow overlooked. Ashley shrugs on the long blond coat and turns the collar up against her chin. Nervously, with a stilted grace he attributes to her high heels, she crosses the kitchen and hugs him. "Simon, you're thinner," she says, her cheek against the front of his shirt. "You're getting to be only skin and bones."

A NOTE ON THE TYPE

This book was set, via computer-driven cathode-ray tube, in Caslon, a modern adaptation of a type designed by the first William Caslon (1692–1766). The Caslon face has had two centuries of ever-increasing popularity in the United States—it is of interest to note that the first copies of the Declaration of Independence and the first paper currency distributed to the citizens of the new-born nation were printed in this typeface.

The book was composed by American–Stratford Graphic Services, Brattleboro, Vermont. It was printed and bound by Fairfield Graphics, Fairfield, Pennsylvania.

Typography and binding design
by Dorothy Schmiderer